Mysterious Rescuer

Connie Griffith and her family live in Boone, North Carolina. She and her husband serve at the headquarters of Africa Evangelical Fellowship. This is her first series of American children's novels.

The Tootie McCarthy Series

BOOK 4

Mysterious Rescuer

Connie Griffith

Baker Books

A Division of Baker Book House Co
Grand Rapids, Michigan 49516

© 1994 by Connie Griffith

Cover illustration by Jim Hsieh, © 1994 Baker Book House

Published by Baker Books
a division of Baker Book House Company
P.O. Box 6287, Grand Rapids, Michigan 49516-6287

Printed in the United States of America

Library of Congress Cataloging-in-Publication Data

Griffith, Connie
    Mysterious rescuer / Connie Griffith
        p. cm. — (The Tootie McCarthy series ; bk. 4)
    Sequel to: Secret behind locked doors.
    Sequel: The shocking discovery.
    Summary: In 1928, after her family moves from St. Paul, Minnesota,
to a farm in Siren, Wisconsin, thirteen-year-old Tootie has trouble
believing that the move is part of God's plan.
    ISBN 0-8010-3865-0
    [1. Irish Americans—Fiction. 2. Family life—Fiction. 3. Moving,
Household—Fiction. 4. Country life—Wisconsin—Fiction. 5. Chris-
tian life—Fiction.] I. Title. II. Series: Griffith, Connie. Tootie
McCarthy series ; bk. 4.
PZ7.G88175My 1994
    [Fic]—dc20   93-8421

Scripture quotations are from the King James Version of the Bible.

To my father,
Arleigh (Arl) Leland Kringle,
who is a consistent example of
kindness and gentle leadership

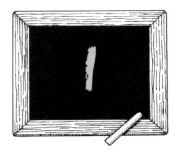

Tootie McCarthy ran the brush through her short reddish-brown curls. She took one last look in the mirror which was propped against the old dresser she shared with her sister and brother.

"I don't feel like doing this," she said to her reflection, trying desperately to gain control of her temper. "Today is February 23, 1928. I'll never forget this day as long as I live!" Then she closed her big hazel eyes and rehearsed for the dozenth time what she was going to say to the reporters.

"For pity's sake, hurry up!" Pearl complained as she came to their bedroom door. "Everyone's waiting. Joey Staddler is already here and so are the people from *The Tribune*. I think the man in the gray flannel suit is some important government official. I bet he's brought along that reward money we heard about!"

Tootie didn't reply and Pearl continued breathlessly, "What do you think, Tootie? Does my hair look good enough for the pictures? What about this dress?"

Finally Tootie turned and stared at her fifteen-year-old sister. Pearl's black shiny hair was parted straight down the middle with both sides coiled and pinned over her ears. Her neatly patched pink dress was definitely too thin for the cold afternoon, but yes, she looked good enough for the pictures. Everything about her sister was pretty, except for her front teeth. But her easygoing attitude over the dreadful events of the past couple of weeks really ground on Tootie's nerves.

"Pearl," Tootie said in a barely controlled tone. "This newspaper interview isn't about you. It's about that awful asylum. It's about our Buddy Boy and how he suffered at their wicked hands!"

"Don't be so dramatic, little sis." Pearl lightly fluffed her puffy sleeves. "All that's behind us now. You rescued Buddy and all the other children out there at that place. You're the famous heroine!"

Tootie wanted to shout, *I'm not the one who should be getting praised. It's all those kids who survived the cruel treatment that should be getting a reward!* But Tootie knew that her older sister didn't want to hear any such thing. So instead she said, "How's Buddy?"

Pearl hesitated for a moment. "Fine, I think."

"Really?" Tootie asked hopefully.

"Sure. That nice Dr. Hargrove came again this morning. I heard him tell Mother and Daddy that Buddy's bruises will heal in a week or two."

Relief flooded Tootie's thin body. "Oh, Pearl, this whole mess has been awful! And I'm so mad at all of us for allowing it to happen to our Buddy Boy."

"It's not our fault!" Pearl defended.

Tootie clenched her fingers together and glared at her sister. "It is *too* our fault! We allowed our little brother to be admitted to that asylum just on the advice of one quack doctor. Oh, Pearl, how could we have done it?"

Pearl stiffened. "But Buddy's different from normal eight-year-olds. And you know Mother couldn't handle him because she's been so sick."

"I know," Tootie moaned. "But I still think we should've been more careful. And . . ." Tootie hesitated, "I'm so upset at the way the newspaper people are making such a big deal out of our tragedy. Just think of what Buddy suffered at the hands of that cruel doctor and nurse at the asylum!"

"Don't tell me." Pearl sighed and pulled on Tootie's arm. "Come out here and tell the reporters. Besides, I'm just positive they're going to give you the reward today." Then Pearl took a deep breath and said quickly before rushing from the room, "Tootie, please give the money to me so I can get my front teeth fixed. *Please!*"

Tootie didn't get a chance to respond. The moment she and Pearl entered the living room of their small family apartment above the Specialty Pie Bakery, everyone cheered.

"Look!" she heard one of the reporters exclaim. "She's just a school girl! How could such a little Irish lass crack a case like this?"

Donald McCarthy lifted his hands and motioned for Tootie to come and join him. "Quiet everyone," he said good-naturedly. "As you've guessed, this is Tootie, our daughter. She's thirteen."

Immediately several floodlights flicked on. Their bright beams with the attached shiny reflectors were directed at Tootie. She squinted. Red, blue, and yellow dots danced wildly in front of her. She could barely make out their dining room table which had been pushed back against the wall. A man, mumbling something, stood behind a big clumsy camera resting on a stand.

As Tootie walked toward her father, she nervously fidgeted with the collar of her brown serge dress. Perspiration popped out on her thin upper lip. She glanced toward the sofa to see how Buddy was reacting to all the bright lights and the heat they made in the already stuffy room. She couldn't see his expression because he was shielding his eyes with his short stubby fingers.

Within a few steps, she reached her father's side. She watched him straighten the lapel of his dark pin-striped suit and smooth to the side his beautifully combed hair with its three waves. He smiled broadly at her, winked, and then turned to the government official and the reporters.

"Tootie told her mother and me that she's feeling— should I say, disturbed and a little nervous about this interview. So let's make it as easy as possible." Father pointed to the floral sofa where Mother, Buddy, and Tootie's best friend, Joey, were sitting. "Come, lass," he said, "sit here next to your brother."

Meanwhile, Pearl had hurried over and perched herself on the arm of the sofa next to Mother.

As Tootie squeezed into her place, she looked searchingly into Buddy's face. He was wrapped in a wool blanket and resting his head on Mother's shoulder. He was still shielding his eyes, but Tootie could see that he looked dreadful. *No way should he be in front of these reporters*, she thought. Her anger bubbled hotly, threatening to choke her.

"Are you all right, Buddy Boy?" Tootie whispered hoarsely. She gently touched his cheek.

Buddy didn't answer in words, but he quickly leaned over and cuddled against her.

Tootie thought this whole thing was cruel. Her family was on display—especially Buddy. She knew the newspaper people wanted to get every detail of the story about the asylum, but she didn't think it was a good idea to have Buddy sit through the interview and be reminded of everything he'd endured. She was anxious to expose the whole asylum scam and get the reward money, but she certainly didn't want her brother hurt anymore than he'd already been.

Joey reached over and touched her arm. She tried to smile, but it faded before it reached her lips.

Immediately a reporter with a notepad began, "Miss McCarthy, what was it that made you suspicious of the Fairbolt asylum?"

"It was that doctor and nurse," Tootie responded, glancing briefly at Buddy and then back at the reporter.

"Can you be more specific?" another reporter requested.

"Well . . . yes. They made a real point of telling us the place did not have bars on the windows. And then when Joey and I went out there to investigate, we found out that was a big lie. There were bars all over the place!"

Just the telling of it made Tootie mad. She clenched her fists. The floodlights seemed to burn brighter.

"Then what happened?" the first reporter asked. "Did you enter the asylum?"

"Yes," Tootie answered, this time without hesitation. "Joey and I had overheard enough to know something awful was going on. We knew we had to get in there and help my brother escape."

"Th-that's right," Joey interrupted. "And when we got inside it was t-terrible. We saw a little boy getting a b-beating!"

The man in the gray suit moved uncomfortably.

Tootie began to feel better about the interview. *This story needs to be told so this kind of thing never happens again*, she thought. With renewed courage she took up the story. "Joey's right. And we could see that most of the children had been beaten. The patients were so frightened that they hid themselves under blankets. That's what we did. Then they marched all of us into a large room and handed out bowls of this awful smelling porridge."

Joey explained about the hairs and probable rat droppings he found in his.

"But the worst thing of all," Tootie concluded and looked lovingly at her little brother, "was the way they mistreated Buddy. They had him tied to the bare boards of his bed. You could tell he'd been beaten because of his swollen face and bruised body."

Tootie hugged Buddy. He looked up into her eyes with a trusting look. The cameraman caught the tender scene.

Joey said, "And when the doctor and nurse discovered Tootie and me . . . they were f-furious! They strapped me to a table and hooked me up to a sh-shock machine. They were experimenting with it on p-patients."

Even the reporters turned pale as they recorded in their notebooks.

"God helped us," Tootie said quickly, remembering Buddy's constant calling out to God, her own prayers for help, and how God used their family and friends to rescue them.

The reporters were starting to question Tootie further when Mother interrupted. Her voice was strained almost beyond recognition. She kept her deep-set eyes on her tightly clasped hands as she said, "We trusted those people—that doctor and that nurse. We admitted our boy into Fairbolt because of their advice. We feel terrible about all that's happened to our son!"

Tootie stared at her mother. This was the first time since Buddy's return that Tootie had heard either of her parents admit how disturbed they were over the whole situation.

"Now listen, Eve," Father said with genuine concern. "You know that you're not well. We thought it was the best thing for our little lad to go to Fairbolt because you've been so sick. You just couldn't take care of Buddy any longer in your condition."

Father stopped and looked around at the reporters.

"My wife has a terrible stomach condition and she's been ill for months. When she got too weak to watch our son and had to stay in bed most of the time, I kept Buddy with me while I worked downstairs in the bakery. That's our family business."

Tootie looked at her parents' tragic faces. Tears burned her eyes.

"What's wrong with your son, Mr. McCarthy?" one of the reporters asked. He'd removed his coat, and he wore wide black suspenders over his slumped shoulders. He held his writing pad, ready to take down every word.

"Our son has a condition called mongolism," Donald replied, brushing moisture from his eyes. "I guess you could say he's retarded."

The camera clicked in Father's face, trying to catch his agony.

Then Father said in a low, tight voice, "The doctor at Fairbolt demanded three thousand dollars in advance!"

Several people in the room gasped. "Where did you get that kind of money, Mr. McCarthy?" the reporter with the wide suspenders asked, looking around at the small, almost shabby apartment.

A red-hot flush crept over Father's neck and face. "I had to borrow against our bakery. It's every bit of money we have."

Tootie's heart hammered hard against her rib cage. *Why did Father have to tell their personal business to these strangers? He's usually so proud. What's happened to him?*

The reporter probed deeper, "Do you think you'll ever see that three thousand again?"

Tootie knew full well that Father had taken the check from the desk at Fairbolt and probably had it hidden away.

"I already have it," Donald admitted. But he didn't offer any further details.

"And you'll have more," the man in the gray flannel suit said as he stood to his feet. He'd been rolling the rim of his derby hat, which he quickly flung onto his chair. "I'm a representative from the governor's office. I'm here to present your daughter with a check for one thousand dollars as a reward for discovering this fraud in our great city of St. Paul, Minnesota."

Everyone could hear Pearl gasp and then clap her dainty hands. Tootie glanced her way, and her older sister's face showed pure delight.

The government official pulled out a piece of paper from his breast pocket. "It's absolutely outrageous that this kind of thing was happening right here under our very noses! We're thankful that this young girl and her friend exposed the terrible Fairbolt asylum scam. And let it be recorded that the doctor and nurse responsible for the mistreatment of the patients are both in jail."

Then he handed the check to Tootie.

The wide shutters on the camera clicked, then clicked again.

"Thank you," Tootie said.

The official nodded proudly, and another picture was taken.

But Tootie's heart sank when he yanked the check right out of her hands and said, "Miss McCarthy, please remove that blanket from your brother. I want you, that little brother of yours, and your accomplice, Joey Staddler, to stand with me over there by the piano. I want to make sure *The Tribune* gets a good picture of all of us. And I'll hold up this thousand-dollar check so the people of this state can see how we reward good citizens."

Tootie only hesitated a moment. *One more picture can't hurt*, she reasoned. Quickly she helped Buddy to his feet and they walked over to the piano to stand next to Joey. After the photo was taken, one of the reporters asked, "What are you going to do with this large amount of money, Miss McCarthy?"

But before Tootie had a chance to reply, Father interrupted. "I've already decided."

Tootie and the rest of the family looked at him in surprise.

"You've made plans with my money?" Tootie asked, barely keeping the reproach out of her voice.

"But I wanted my front teeth fixed," Pearl whispered on the verge of tears.

Mother must have been frowning because Father said, "Don't worry, Eve. You'll like it."

Buddy leaned against Tootie. She put her arm around him and then looked over at Joey. He shrugged.

"I'm sure we'll discuss this later as a family," Mother said and smiled around at the reporters.

"That's all right, dear," Donald said. "I don't mind. I'll tell everyone the good news." He stood in front of the crowd and said proudly, "I've decided to buy us a farm. That's right . . . we're moving! The McCarthy family is moving!"

"Moving!" Tootie shouted. Then she shut her mouth tight. She didn't trust herself to say another word.

Immediately after Donald McCarthy's announcement about moving, the reporters flicked off their floodlights and the cameraman began to take down his stand and put everything away in his big canvas carryall.

For a few seconds longer the red, blue, and yellow spots continued to bounce before Tootie's eyes. Her head throbbed. Pearl ran into their bedroom, while Buddy hurried over to the sofa. Mother covered him as he curled up under his brown blanket.

It was obvious that even the reporters thought their task was finished and they were mumbling among themselves about getting the story and pictures down to the headquarters and then leaving for their next assignment.

The government official shook hands with Tootie's parents and made his final farewell to the reporters before putting on his derby and hurrying out of the apartment to the parked Model T below.

She heard the reporters grumbling about the official's fancy new automobile, and another's complaint about how government officials were actually the people's servants and shouldn't be spending so much money.

But Tootie wasn't interested in their gossip. She wanted to talk to someone about her father's terrible announcement.

"Can you stay for a little while?" Tootie asked as Joey slipped into his black-and-white plaid jacket.

"Sorry, Tootie," Joey said with a distressed look. He plopped his hat toward the back of his head. "My dad d-didn't want me to miss school even for this newspaper interview. But once I promised I'd get right b-back after it finished, he agreed. I'm sure he's st-standing out there watching to see if I do as I promised."

The Staddlers lived directly across the busy city street from the McCarthys. Joey's parents owned the grocery store, and Joey was probably right—Mr. Staddler was no doubt watching out his window to see if his son would obey. He'd been particularly upset lately, claiming that his son was getting into trouble since he'd become such good friends with the youngest McCarthy girl.

Tootie leaned against the open apartment door to watch her best friend descend the outside steps. When Joey reached Washington Street, he turned and waved. Then he glanced across the traffic, and even with a trolley bus passing, Mr. Staddler could be seen peering out his store window. Quickly Joey pulled up the collar of his coat against the cold February wind and hurried down the boardwalk to Logan School.

Tootie stood there for a long time until her parents

complained, "You're letting in all that cold air. Shut the door."

She didn't slam it, but Tootie shut the door decisively harder than necessary. "I'll take Buddy into the bedroom and get him out of his good clothes," she offered.

Tootie had always shown her father great respect, but the idea of him making a life-changing decision such as a move—and with her reward money—was more than she could handle. She wanted to be away from him before she said something she'd regret.

"Toot . . . Toot . . . Toot," Buddy said from the sofa and stretched out his arms.

He looked exhausted and Tootie's heart immediately softened. "Come, Buddy Boy," she said. "Why don't you get into your pajamas and take a nap?"

Mother was rearranging the dining room table and chairs, trying to get the apartment in order. Tootie noticed that she too looked exhausted. She had improved under the care of their new doctor, but she still wasn't completely back to full strength. Her gray hair was pulled into its usual low bun and her deep-set eyes looked almost lost in the dark circles surrounding them. *Father's announcement hasn't set well with her either,* Tootie thought.

Before leading Buddy from the room, Tootie glanced over toward the old, out-of-tune piano to make sure her thousand-dollar check was still on top. She hadn't really taken the time to examine it closely. But she had noticed all those zeros.

The moment Tootie and Buddy entered the bedroom,

they heard Pearl sobbing into her pillow on the double bed where she was sprawled. Tootie quickly shut the bedroom door.

"Oh, Tootie," Pearl immediately pleaded, looking up at her. "Don't give your money to anyone else but me. I've just got to get my teeth fixed! This is my last chance. We'll never have this much money ever again!" Pearl buried her face in her pillow again and continued crying.

Years earlier Pearl's front teeth had broken and their parents never had enough money to replace the temporary plastic teeth that a dentist had made for her. They didn't look too bad, Tootie thought, but Pearl was constantly complaining about them saying they marred her good looks.

"I really hadn't decided what I was going to do with my money," Tootie said honestly. "But I can tell you one thing . . . I definitely don't want to move to some old farm!"

"Me either," Pearl said on a sob. "But I've been thinking Tootie . . . Daddy couldn't have been serious. I think he was just teasing to stop those reporters from getting nosy. You know how he can be. He loves to tease."

"I bet you're right!" There was great relief in Tootie's voice as she helped Buddy out of his flannel shirt and corduroy knickerbockers. "Why didn't I think of that before? Sure, he must've been teasing! Now, that makes more sense."

"Besides," Pearl continued and wiped her eyes, "I'm sure he'd never want to move away from our bakery and

live on some farm! Neither would I! The whole idea
gives me the creeps! No, Daddy was just teasing to stop
them from questioning you about the thousand-dollar
reward money."

"I hope you're right."

"Sure I am." Pearl dried her tears. "Please, Tootie,
don't let anyone decide for you about your money . . .
not even Daddy. He'll probably want to use it to get
some new equipment for the bakery, or help pay for all
that new medicine that Dr. Hargrove is giving Mama."

Tootie didn't say a word.

"Give it to me for my teeth," Pearl pleaded. "Please!"

"I could do that," Tootie said.

"Really?"

"Well, sure . . . why not? I think there would be plenty
left over for some other things. I'd like—"

Pearl jumped up, interrupting Tootie's comment. She
gave her little sister a huge hug. "Will you really do that
for me?" Pearl cried. Then she hugged Tootie again,
and then Buddy. He hugged back and smiled, uncer-
tain of what was going on.

"I'm going to get my teeth fixed . . . I'm going to get
my teeth fixed!" Pearl sang excitedly as she continued
squeezing Tootie and Buddy and then dancing around
in circles.

Tootie laughed. She'd never seen her sister so happy.
She knew Pearl had tried to get money in the past to
pay for a dentist, but nothing ever worked out.

Even Buddy was beginning to laugh and jump
around. The stress of the past days at the asylum seemed

to slide away from him. That terrible doctor and nurse at Fairbolt had shaved Buddy's head, which he now jerked back and forth as he copied the antics of their older sister. Buddy looked more like his usual happy self, and joy flooded Tootie's whole being. She too joined in the fun.

Everything's going to work out after all, she thought, and continued dancing in circles with Buddy and Pearl.

That evening around the supper table, Buddy was absent. He still hadn't awakened from his nap and it was decided it would be best to let him sleep.

Mother was making a remarkable recovery from her stomach ailment and the improvement in her health was obvious to all. "That new medicine Dr. Hargrove is giving me is really helping," Eve said as she sat down in her usual place at the opposite end of the table from Father. "My stomach cramps are gone, and I'm actually hungry for the first time in weeks."

"That's great news," Donald said.

Mother continued, "I must admit that I was quite exhausted this morning after that interview with the reporters, but I'm feeling much better now."

Donald smiled. "They certainly were a nosey lot."

Tootie and Pearl looked at each other. *Pearl's right,* Tootie thought. *Father was just teasing. We're not moving!* "Isn't your mother looking grand?" Father continued and nodded at Pearl and then at Tootie.

They both agreed.

"Honestly, Mama," Tootie said, "it's almost as if a miracle has happened to you."

"In a way it has," Eve responded. "We certainly were praying for one. God knew we were all stretched to the limit with my poor health . . . and then Buddy's ordeal at that asylum. Anyway," she said more cheerfully, "I believe all of this is behind us now. Everything's going to be fine."

Pearl said happily, "It sure is!" and winked at Tootie and then pointed to her front teeth.

"That's right," Donald added. "Life will be better from here on out." He smiled around the table at his family. "Evelyn McCarthy, will you please give thanks for this delicious meal before it gets cold?"

They all bowed their heads. While Mother said grace, Tootie whispered her own prayer of thanksgiving. This was the best life had been in a long, long time.

The cherry wood of the dining room table was covered with a freshly starched and pressed Irish linen tablecloth. Even the cloth napkins had been laundered and they lay stiffly next to the fine china place settings. And to make the dinner more perfect, Mother had added a little more ham than usual to their boiled cabbage and ham dinner. There was even plenty of vinegar in their fancy cruet. *Yes, this is the best it's been in a very long time*, Tootie thought.

As soon as the prayer was finished, Mother said, "I haven't seen that thousand-dollar check. I looked for it this afternoon as I was picking up around the apartment. Wasn't it left on the piano, Donald?"

"Certainly," Father replied happily as he began spooning the cabbage and ham onto the first plate and passing it down to Mother. "I told Tootie I'd put it in a safe place. Don't worry." Then he spooned another plateful and gave it to Pearl and then one to Tootie. Finally he served himself. They all waited until Mother took the first bite before they began.

"When do you think our picture will be in the newspaper?" Tootie asked.

Father chuckled. "Anxious to see yourself in the news?"

"Don't tease," Eve admonished with a smile. "Naturally Tootie is excited about how this whole ordeal concerning the asylum has turned out. It's one of those incidences where God changes all the bad things around for good."

"And this is certainly one of those times," Pearl said and took a hearty mouthful.

"All right," Father agreed, "I won't do any more teasing, at least not for the next few minutes anyway." He smiled at Tootie.

Tootie beamed. She felt happier than she'd felt in months. It seemed like suddenly everything was going right: Her family was getting along; the terrible tension over their creeping poverty was now behind them due to her reward money; Mother's health was miraculously improving; and even Buddy was sleeping soundly in his own bed and not in some awful asylum.

"The reporters said they were hoping to get the picture and article in today's paper," Father was explaining. "It's probably in there right now. I'll go down to the street after we finish eating and buy a copy."

"You could buy dozens of copies with all the money we've got," Pearl said and let out a little laugh.

The remainder of the meal was pleasant. Father mostly talked, and he brought up incidences in their lives before they'd moved to Minnesota and purchased the Specialty Pie Bakery. He loved talking about the days when they were rich, whenever he got in a good mood.

"Remember, Eve, how you used to fix roast lamb?" Father smiled down the table.

"Yes, dear, I remember," Mother answered. "You always liked to eat it with a mint sauce, didn't you?"

"That's right!" Then Father looked at Tootie. "Who knows what's ahead? Maybe more lamb!"

Tootie laughed. "Maybe even two!" She loved the feeling of having the power to make people happy. She wanted to buy half a dozen sheep if that would keep her father in this wonderful mood.

After the meal, Father brought in *The Tribune*. He quickly opened it on the cleared dining room table and began scanning the pages. "Here it is!" he announced when he got to page three. He pointed to the picture of Tootie, Buddy, Joey, and the government official holding the one-thousand-dollar reward check high above their heads. The caption read in bold print: **13-year-old Cracks the Fairbolt Asylum Scam**.

"That's a great picture of you, Tootie," Pearl said.

Tootie looked at the picture. It was pretty good of her

and Joey, but her heart ached as she stared at the picture of Buddy. He looked almost frightening with his shaved head and bruised face. And for some reason he had let his tongue hang out when they had taken the photo. It looked terrible. Tears burned her eyes. *No one will ever understand how sweet he is by looking at this picture.*

The article told it all. The reporters had done a thorough job. Tootie and Joey were made out to be true heroes, especially Tootie. She even liked the sound of the words in the article, and for the first time she began to feel genuinely good about the situation. She and Joey had really helped the whole town by exposing the fraud at Fairbolt. Everything was perfect except for that awful picture of Buddy.

Then Father pointed to another article on the same page and began to read it out loud. It was about the necessity of having asylums and the service they provided in keeping crazy people off the streets. It went on to explain the need to keep the retarded separated from normal people.

Tootie jumped to her feet and shouted, "What are we going to do? That makes Buddy out to be some sort of dangerous person who needs to be kept locked up!"

"Not so," Father said. "This article is obviously prejudiced, no one will pay it any attention, and they certainly won't link it to our Buddy. I don't think we need to be one bit concerned."

Eve agreed. "Father's right. No one will pay any heed to the article. That debate over asylums and who should be in them is old news. Don't give it a second thought, dear. But this news," and Eve pointed to the article about the Fairbolt scam, "is what's going to catch all the attention."

But Tootie wasn't satisfied. "What if people think Buddy's crazy just because of the way he looks?"

Eve looked at her distraught daughter. "You can't stop people from talking, lass. There will always be folks who judge others by their looks . . . and those who even mistreat them."

"But after meeting our boy," Father concluded in a lighter tone, "no one would believe for a minute that he's crazy or deserves to be in an asylum. So don't worry. It's obvious that he's a kind little boy. I agree, this picture of him isn't very good . . . but it won't do any harm."

"Besides," Mother said, "everyone around here already knows Buddy, and the article explains clearly how we were fooled into admitting him into that awful place. So quit your worrying. I'm sure that no harm will come from that other article."

"I guess you're right," Tootie finally conceded. "At least Buddy's safe here and most people who come into our bakery are used to him."

"Why don't we all go over and get comfortable on the davenport and chair," Father quickly suggested. "I have some good news to tell you."

"You have been looking rather excited," Mother commented and touched his arm.

"What is it?" Pearl asked. She put her hand to the

side of her mouth and whispered to Tootie, "Maybe he's thought about my teeth and he's already found a good dentist."

Tootie giggled as she sat down on the sofa between Mother and Pearl. Father sat opposite them in the overstuffed chair. Everything seemed so perfect.

"You all know that I got a loan against our bakery to pay that large fee at Fairbolt," Father began.

They all nodded.

"It was three thousand dollars. Well . . . when you add that to the one-thousand-dollar reward that Tootie just received, what do you get?"

"Four thousand," Mother said with some reserve. "But—"

Donald held up his hand to interrupt. "Let me finish, Eve. I've asked myself over and over, when will I ever have that much money again? And the answer is, never. Never again! I've given this whole situation a lot of thought." He paused and took a deep breath. "As you all are aware, our bakery business is failing."

Tootie felt a lump form in her throat. She knew things were bad, but not that bad!

Then Father looked directly at her and then at Pearl. "And you both recognize that your mother has not been well. She is improving, for which we are grateful," and he smiled at Eve, "but she still needs rest. And then there's Buddy . . . he shouldn't be cooped up in this small apartment above some rundown bakery!"

"Now, Donald," Mother began, "things are not all that bad."

Father lifted his hand again to ward off more inter-ruption. "They have been bad, Eve, there's no denying. I went to the bank and turned in the deed to our business. The bakery is no longer ours. We'll have no more worries on that end. I've already dismissed our baker."

Mother's face turned deathly white. "What are we going to do? What have you done with all that money?"

"I already told you, Eve. I even announced it to the reporters."

"But I didn't think you were serious!" Mother said.

"Of course I'm serious! I've combined the three thou-sand we got for the business with Tootie's reward money. I've bought us a farm and a second-hand truck. We're actually moving!"

Tootie's heart pounded and her head felt like it was going to burst wide open.

Pearl began to cry.

Just then Buddy came walking out of the bedroom. All of the noise and excitement must have disturbed him. Besides, he'd been asleep most of the day. He stood at the end of the sofa in his blue pajamas. He let his small shaved head lean to the left and he grinned sheep-ishly around at his family. A dark stain could be seen down the front of his pajama bottoms. He had wet his pants.

What's a move going to do to him? Tootie asked her-self. *Or to the rest of us?* She looked at Pearl who was now sobbing into one of the cushions on the sofa, and then at Mother. The worry-lines between her eyebrows seemed to deepen and the tired look she had had earlier returned.

Anger burned in Tootie's soul. *How can this be happening? How can Father do this? How can he spend my reward money without asking me?* She had never felt such anger. *What am I going to do?*

Eve stood slowly to her feet. "Donald," she said with a frown between her deep-set eyes, "we know absolutely *nothing* about farming. What in the world possessed you to buy a farm?"

Mother had never challenged Father's decisions, at least not in front of the family. Tootie held her breath.

To everyone's surprise, Father smiled without a hint of irritation. "We can't go wrong on this one, Eve. There's a bill before Congress at this very moment. It promises that the government will pay farmers for their crops. Our new farm is bound to be a great success. Here, read some of these articles for yourself."

Eve looked skeptical as she reached across and took the offered newspaper. "Lots of things are written in *The Tribune*, Donald."

Tootie remembered the article which had made a case for having asylums. Her anger increased. Donald stood and put his arms tenderly around Eve. "Don't worry," he said. "You and Buddy will enjoy the country. I think farm life will suit the both of you."

Father was probably right. However, Tootie couldn't imagine her father living on a farm; he couldn't be less suited to country life. And neither was Pearl. *And I just don't want to move*, Tootie thought rebelliously.

"Sit down, lad," Father said to Buddy. "Sit right here on this blanket." Father patted Buddy on the shoulder and then pointed to the brown wool blanket that had been left on the floor after the interview that morning.

"I should go get him into some dry clothes," Mother said. She still held the newspaper Father had given her and it looked like she had no intention of reading it.

"Not just yet," Donald responded. "Changing Buddy can wait. I want you to see something first. And you, too," he said to Tootie and Pearl. "And please dry those tears, Pearl. This isn't as bad as you think. It'll be great!"

Pearl looked up. Huge tears filled her eyes and her lips trembled. "Does this mean I can't get my teeth fixed?" Her voice was barely more than a whisper.

The look of lost hope on Pearl's face was heartbreaking to see.

"Your what?" Father asked.

"Her teeth!" Tootie shouted.

Mother quickly intervened. "It's obvious, Donald, that our daughters discussed how some of the reward money was going to be spent. And I must say . . . that was certainly thoughtful of you, Tootie, to consider your sister's teeth." There was a strained smile on Mother's face as she nodded at Tootie and then at Pearl.

"Maybe we could manage that, too," Father suggested.

But Tootie could tell by his manner and the way he

said it that he had no intention whatsoever of following through on that promise. This upcoming move was totally preoccupying his mind, and it would probably take every penny they had.

Pearl obviously concluded the same because she started crying all over again.

"Just wait till you read this," Father said with growing excitement, ignoring the tears from Pearl, the angry glares from Tootie, and the irritated expression all over Mother's face. He pulled a piece of paper from his pocket, spreading it flat on the coffee table. It was a cutout advertisement from the newspaper. One whole section was underlined.

Tootie and Pearl leaned close to see. Even Mother sat down and leaned forward. The underlined words announced:

COZY FARMHOUSE ON 40 ACRES OF PRIME LAND IN SIREN, WISCONSIN. JUST $2,750! BARN AND COW, "BABE," INCLUDED.

Father rubbed his hands together. "Sounds perfect, doesn't it? I've already paid for the farm, and the remaining amount went for a truck. It's a great opportunity, Eve. Things like this come just once in a lifetime."

Father leaned over close to Buddy. "Let me tell you something, lad. We own a cow. Her name's Babe."

"Babe . . . Babe . . . Babe," Buddy repeated. Then he let his tongue hang out and continued rubbing the brown blanket between his fingers.

Tootie's fist came down hard on the coffee table. "Where is Siren, Wisconsin?"

Father looked at her in surprise.

Tootie glared back.

Finally Father answered, "It's ninety-seven miles away. And what in the world's wrong with you, lass? I've never seen you so upset."

Tootie's cheeks burned. She knew she shouldn't keep glaring at her father in such a manner, but anger boiled inside her. *How could he not even know?*

Mother intervened, "I want you two girls to get Buddy changed and then do the dishes." She looked sternly at Tootie and then at Pearl. "I'm putting an end to this family discussion right now. None of us want to say anything in anger. You can never take back words once they've been spoken."

Pearl darted into the bedroom, slamming the door behind her. Tootie grabbed Buddy's hand and led him from the room, grumbling every step of the way.

Later that evening Tootie and Pearl did the dishes in silence. They were both trying to hear the conversation going on between their parents in the other room.

"The sooner we leave, the better," Father was saying. "We could start packing right away and get everything onto the truck in a day or so."

"Donald," Eve protested, "I don't believe . . ." But from the kitchen, neither Tootie nor Pearl could hear her quiet response. Then Mother continued a little louder, "What about you, Donald? You've never been near a farm. Will you know what to do?"

Father chuckled. "I'll learn. We'll all learn. It'll be a great challenge! We were bound to lose our bakery sooner or later. This is a good way out for us. We're just plain lucky. We got out before the business completely folded."

Eve responded, "I don't know if luck has anything to do with it, Donald."

Tootie knew Mother didn't believe in luck. She often said, "We make our own way in life by hard work, trust in God, and stick-to-itiveness. There's no such thing as the luck of the Irish."

"It sure wasn't luck," Tootie whispered to Pearl while vigorously scrubbing the chipped enamel saucepan that had been used for the cabbage and ham. "That reward money was mine. I earned it!"

"And you were going to give some to me," Pearl said with a pathetic look.

Tootie quickly hugged her older sister. Water and soap suds dripped onto the floor from Tootie's wet hands. But neither of the McCarthy sisters noticed.

Not another word was said about the upcoming move for the rest of the evening. Everyone went to bed early almost as if by ignoring the facts, they would go away.

Early the next morning when Tootie and Pearl got up to go to school, they discovered their home in a state of total disarray. Clothes from their parents' bedroom were folded in piles by the bedroom door, dishes were stacked on the dining room table, and even the cushions from the sofa and chair were piled high against the far wall by the piano.

Mother was alone in the dining room and she looked up from packing her good china in a box. "Get yourselves a couple of slices of bread to eat," she greeted. "Then start packing your own things."

It felt as if the floor had been knocked out from underneath Tootie. She couldn't believe they were actually going through with this move. She thought her mother would have somehow talked Father out of it or at least made him come to a point where he was willing to reconsider. Everything was happening too fast. She hadn't even had a chance to talk with Joey. What was she going to do without her best friend?

"I can see you both are stunned," Mother said kindly. "I realize this has all come as quite a surprise. It has to me, too. But your father has thought everything through. He's been planning this move from the moment we brought Buddy home from the asylum. He notified the bank that he wanted to keep the three thousand he'd borrowed against the business and turn over the bakery to them. Then he contacted some real estate company and purchased that Wisconsin farm we read about."

"I can't believe it!" Tootie said. She angrily wrapped her robe tighter, staring down at her bare toes. The floor was cold because her parents always turned the heat down during the night.

"We're really moving?" Pearl asked, dumfounded. "Just like that?"

"Yes," Mother said. "I guess your father thought it would be easier if things happened fast. Anyway, he decided that a move to a farm would be the best thing for all of us. And then with your reward money, Tootie, he was also able to buy a truck and make all the final arrangements. There's just a little money left over for whatever we'll need to set up our new life on the farm."

Tootie stiffened.

Pearl let out a little whimper.

"By the way, Tootie, that reward check was made out to your father. That's how he was able to cash it. The truck's parked down on Washington Street. I think we'll be able to finish packing today, and leave for Siren, Wisconsin, first thing tomorrow morning."

"Tomorrow?" both girls gasped.

Eve nodded. "Your father's at Logan School right now getting your reports, so it should be easy to transfer to one of the schools in Siren. He's also saying our good-byes to the pastor. We're going to miss him."

Tootie agreed, still staring down at her cold bare toes.

"Your father's also arranged for a buyer to come and take away the rest of the supplies from the bakery. He really has thought of just about everything."

"Except my teeth," Pearl added under her breath.

Tootie didn't want to hear anymore. She hurried into the kitchen.

All day they packed. It was incredible how quickly their family apartment became stripped of all that made it home. They were just finishing when Joey knocked on the door.

"I've come to help," he said to Tootie as he entered the apartment. His plaid jacket was buttoned up tight against the chilly evening, and his nose was red from the cold. He rubbed his hands together as he said, "I c-can't believe you're moving!"

"Me either!" Tootie responded with obvious anger.

"I-I would have come earlier, but my dad had me d-delivering groceries after school."

Before they could say any more to each other, or even say a proper good-bye, Tootie's father came in. "Glad to see you, young man. Will you give me a hand with this davenport?"

The remainder of the evening Joey helped. By nighttime all the beds, mattresses, table and chairs, piano, sofa, and dressers were loaded onto the truck with many boxes. Everything was covered with dozens of old blankets donated by neighbors, and the whole load was tied securely.

That night the McCarthy family slept on a quilt in the middle of their living room floor. Tootie didn't actually sleep. Basically she tossed and turned on the quilt, which was little protection from the hardwood floor.

This is my last night in the city, she thought. *What in the world will tomorrow bring?* She socked the quilt with her balled fist, hating the feeling of being helpless to stop the fast-moving events that were overtaking them.

I mustn't go to sleep! Maybe I should go down and do

something to our load of furniture . . . maybe even the truck. I have to do something to stop us from leaving in the morning!

But total exhaustion from the day's work settled over Tootie like a heavy cape, and soon she was sound asleep.

The entire McCarthy family got up early the next morning while it was still dark outside. The apartment was empty and cold as Tootie walked from room to room for the last time in the only home she had ever known.

She followed her parents down to the pie bakery to make a final check. It looked so different with cleared-off shelves, clean counters and display case, and not even a whiff of pastry baking in the big ovens. A "For Sale" sign was propped against the front window, with the bank phone number written neatly underneath.

With growing emotions, Tootie hurried out to the loaded truck. Pearl and Buddy were already there. Almost immediately their parents joined them. Tootie didn't even look their way.

They could all crowd into the front of the truck instead of someone sitting on top of the load of furniture, but they had to decide who would sit on whom.

"It's entirely too cold this hour of the morning for anyone to sit back there," Mother insisted. "Besides it's dangerous! We're all just going to have to squeeze closer together."

Pearl pouted. "For ninety-seven miles!"

Tootie didn't like the idea any better than Pearl. But what else could they do? Somewhat begrudgingly she suggested, "Why doesn't Buddy sit on my lap? And, Pearl, if you scoot forward and sit on the edge of the seat, there may be enough room."

Everyone began rearranging themselves.

"This is embarrassing," Pearl continued to complain. "What if someone sees us traveling like this?"

Who cares! Tootie grumbled to herself. Her anger was growing deeper by the second.

As Father started to pull away from the curb on Washington Street, Tootie looked around the familiar street for the last time. To her total surprise, Joey was standing next to the vinegar keg by the front door of his parents' store. He wasn't waving; he was just standing there looking at them. It was still dark, and Tootie knew she wouldn't have seen Joey if it hadn't been for the headlights on the truck.

"Stop!" Tootie hollered.

Father slammed on the brakes, and the whole load shifted. "I've had enough from you two!" Donald shouted at Tootie and Pearl. "This packing and getting everything ready has been hard enough. Not another word from either one of you!"

Pearl huffed. Buddy leaned against Tootie and began to cry.

"But—" Tootie began to explain.

"Silence!" Donald shouted.

Tootie didn't think her father had seen Joey, but even if he had, Tootie doubted he would let her say goodbye. She'd never heard her father raise his voice so loudly.

Tootie stared wide-eyed at the figure of Joey as they drove away. She would have been shocked if she'd seen the tears coursing down his cheeks.

The next hours dragged by for Tootie. Buddy fell sound asleep on her lap. Pearl leaned forward and rested her head on the dash, while Mother dozed on Father's shoulder. The truck lumbered on down the highway toward Siren, Wisconsin, and farther and farther away from home.

Tootie could not relax. And she definitely didn't want to make small talk with her father. Questions swirled round and round in her head as she sat in stony silence. *Will I ever have another friend? What will the farm be like? What school will I go to?* She was afraid, but her fears only added to the seething anger she still felt over this whole situation.

Just then Buddy moaned and snuggled closer to her chest. She tugged on his brown blanket, which Pearl was sitting on, so that she could wrap it around Buddy and make him more comfortable. The truck had flaps that snapped down, instead of side windows. Tootie felt chilled to the bone. She tried pulling Buddy even closer to help keep them both warm. As the day progressed, to their great dismay, they began to see snow. It was packed firmly, as if it had been there all winter. A few flakes began to fall and the road felt icy. Finally they pulled over to the side of Highway 35 for Father to check the load. Everything was securely tied, but the snow was beginning to soak through the blankets that covered their furniture. Father mumbled something as he got back into the truck.

Tootie thought for sure she heard him swear.

Mother said quickly, "Sandwiches, anyone?" She reached into a small basket which the church ladies had provided. On almost any other occasion, Tootie would have loved a scrambled egg sandwich with bits of onion and green pepper—but not today. A cold egg sandwich sounded awful. She took one anyway.

Buddy had awakened with all the commotion of checking the load. He took a sandwich, and it wasn't long before greasy pieces of onion and egg were falling out of the sandwich and all down the front of his coat and even onto Tootie.

"Quit making such a mess!" Pearl complained. But she didn't try to help.

Suddenly the thought of introducing her brother to total strangers made Tootie gag. *What if they make fun of him? What if they ask about his shaved head and bruises? I don't want anyone ever to find out our Buddy was in an asylum,* Tootie determined. *I'll keep it a secret!* she vowed to herself and also to Buddy, who was munching contentedly on his sandwich.

The McCarthys stopped several times along the way in hopes that the weather would improve. But it didn't. The snow kept falling. Around three in the afternoon they finally approached the outskirts of Siren. They had to turn off the main highway to get to the town. The moment they did, their truck began to swerve back and forth on the icy country road. Father was convinced that their heavy load was keeping them from sliding completely into the ditch on either side.

"I've been given some instructions," Donald said loudly, not taking his eyes nor his concentration off the road. "The people from the realty office told me to locate the Siren Shinler Mercantile as soon as I drove into town."

Buddy had fallen back to sleep. Tootie tried to motion for her father to keep his voice a little quieter, so as not to wake Buddy. She knew all the swerving on the roads would scare him. But Father obviously didn't see her.

"I understand," Donald continued in his tense, loud voice, "that Mr. Shinler, the owner of the store, will give us directions to our new farm. But I have no idea where this store is located."

"Didn't he tell you?" Mother asked.

"No. When I asked, the realtor just laughed and said, 'You'll see the store; you can't miss it!'"

"They must have a big sign," Pearl offered.

"Or maybe it's the only store in town," Mother added, trying not to show how apprehensive she'd become.

Throughout the entire conversation, Buddy remained asleep. They all became silent as Father ground the gears of the truck into low and proceeded slowly down Main Street. On the left, there was a gas station, a butcher shop, and a run-down post office. On the right stood a bank and a small church with the white paint peeling off. There was a sign in front, which hung at an angle. It had one word—WELCOME.

Father ground the gears again. "Sounds like the clutch bands are wearing out," he said to no one in particular.

As they slowly moved down the second block, they saw a small house on the left with a tarnished brass sign by the front door. It read: DR. TREADWELL. And next to the doctor's was a bakery that looked like it had long ago gone out of business. Across the street stood a big wooden building painted brown with a sign above the door: SHINLER MERCANTILE. Under the red lettering was written: Town Hall (upstairs). Next to the Mercantile was a weathered frame boardinghouse. And next to this was a train depot at the edge of town.

"I guess this is it," Father said. His voice was very low.

"Do you mean this is the entire town?" Pearl's voice held a note of hysteria.

No one answered her question. It was obvious. Father pulled up in front of the Shinler Mercantile. Goods of all kinds were stacked in the wide front display windows of the store.

"I should go in and ask directions to our farm," Father said. His voice sounded strained.

"I'll go with you," Tootie offered. Besides, her legs and back side felt numb.

Mother sighed. "Be careful, you two. It's awful slick out there, and you aren't wearing boots."

Tootie pushed the sleeping Buddy off her lap and got out of the truck. The cold air immediately set her to shivering, and she hung onto Father as they hurried into the store.

A potbellied stove stood in the center of the room with rocking chairs and two short benches surrounding it. Several customers in old work coats were warming their hands by the fire, and they looked up as Tootie and Donald entered.

The smell of the crackling wood, plus the unfamiliar odors of the fabrics, leather goods, tools, and the black licorice and cinnamon sticks in the jars near the cash register made Tootie's stomach turn. The smells didn't set at all well with the egg sandwich she'd eaten earlier.

"Can I help?" a man behind the cash register asked as he scratched his balding head.

"I hope so," Father replied. He pulled a paper from his suit coat. "I'm Donald McCarthy. I have a letter here from my realtor in Minnesota. He says that you will give me directions to the farm I just purchased."

"So you're the city slicker who bought that old place," one of the customers by the fire commented. He spit a dark stream of tobacco juice into a tin cup and grinned. The others grinned, while looking the newcomers up and down.

And my father bought it with my reward money, Tootie could have added. But, of course, she didn't. In fact, she was beginning to feel a little sorry for her father. He looked extremely uncomfortable and out of place amid these country folk.

The man behind the register jabbed his thumb toward his friends. "Don't mind them," he said. "We've all been curious about who bought that old place—especially at this time of year." He stopped and looked out the store window at the falling snow.

Father mumbled something under his breath. Then he straightened the lapels of his suit and said, "Just give me the directions."

Tootie turned and looked out the window when suddenly she saw the strangest sight. A yellow school bus with the words "SIREN CONSOLIDATED SCHOOLS" written in black along the side, came into view. The bus itself wasn't so funny. But the tires had been removed and it rested on long metal runners. It was being pulled to a halt on the icy road in front of the store by a team of wild-looking horses.

"Look!" Tootie shouted and then laughed.

Donald leaned forward and looked out the dirty windows. "Well, I've never!" He squinted his eyes as if he couldn't believe what he was seeing. Then he put his derby back onto his wavy hair and chuckled. "Well, lass, welcome to the country!"

The Siren folks stiffened. "Don't see anything funny," one of the customers said as he leaned forward and stared out the window. Then he reached toward the door. Before he pushed it open, he said over his shoulder to the man behind the register, "Hey, Shinler, here comes your girl. See you tomorrow."

Tootie quickly looked to see the storekeeper's daughter. *Maybe we can be friends*, she thought.

Just then a girl about twice Tootie's size emerged from the bus. She had a ridiculous abundance of black curls sticking out from under her purple knit cap. She wore a purple coat and gloves to match. Tootie had never seen such an outfit, not even on the richest girl in the city. The storeowner's daughter had rosy cheeks and bright red lips.

Tootie felt certain that this girl's vivid coloring was not natural. Instantly, she was disappointed. Then something much more than disappointment began to well up inside her. *This overdressed country girl is nothing compared to my city friends*, Tootie thought. Suddenly all her frustration and anger over the move settled upon the purple-clad girl, who was sauntering slowly down the bus steps.

Tootie balled her fists.

Then to her surprise, a short simple-looking boy appeared at the bus door. He was about nine years old, and he looked a lot like Buddy, except his eyes were crossed. He wore an old pair of overalls and two flannel shirts. He didn't even have on a coat, hat, or boots. He said something, and it was obvious that he slobbered when he talked. Tootie's heart ached for the little fellow. *Who is he? What's he trying to say?*

Just then Tootie saw the storeowner's daughter turn and laugh at the boy. She began chanting loudly in a singsong tone, "Olof's a dumb head; Olof's a dumb head!" She twirled her purple gloved hands around in a circle by her head and tried to cross her eyes.

Several of the kids inside the bus began to laugh. Tootie could see them.

Little Olof began to cry.

It was too much for Tootie. All the anger and frustration over the move, plus all her protective feelings for Buddy, overwhelmed her. Tootie swung open the front door of the Mercantile and darted out into the cold afternoon. She ran right up to the Shinler girl and shoved her. Hard!

The surprised girl screamed, lost her balance, and fell facedown in the snow.

"Leave that boy alone!" Tootie shouted.

The shocked Shinler girl looked up at her assailant with snow-covered face and lashes, and with her lipstick smeared half way across her cheek.

The kids in the bus stared, and some even leaned out to get a closer look.

The horses reared, their eyes were wild; their nostrils flared.

"Who's the new girl?" she heard someone shout. "Beats me!" another answered. "But Sylvia Shinler's finally met her match!"

What have I done? Tootie thought in horror.

Within seconds, Father and Mr. Shinler were at Tootie's side. Even Pearl came to help. Mother stayed in the truck with Buddy, who was still sound asleep.

In a gallant manner, Father stretched out his hand toward Sylvia Shinler and said in a dignified, but exaggerated tone, "You must have slipped, young lady. It certainly is icy. Here, let me give you a helping hand."

Tootie felt pretty certain that Father knew what had really happened and was secretly enjoying every minute of it.

"I didn't slip!" Sylvia shouted in total outrage, pointing her purple-gloved finger at Tootie. "She pushed me!"

"That's right," Tootie admitted, almost defiantly. Then she straightened her slender shoulders, which were now sprinkled with falling snow. "I had to. She was teasing that poor boy."

Tootie motioned toward Olof, who was still crying. He stood on the top step of the bus. It was obvious that Olof had a hard time controlling his saliva as he slob-

bered down the front of his flannel shirts. A tall handsome boy, who looked about fourteen, had joined Olof
and was standing protectively by his side.

"Sylvia, inside!" Mr. Shinler shouted. He jabbed his
thumb toward the Mercantile.

"But Pa—" Sylvia whined.

"Now!" he hollered.

Sylvia dusted off her purple coat and glared at Tootie.
"You just wait," she snarled under her breath as she
passed.

Pearl squeezed Tootie's hand.

Then Mr. Shinler hollered to the boy standing next
to Olof, "Hey, Arl, are you and your pa working out at
the Olson place?"

"Yes, sir," Arl replied.

"Then you'd better take care of that lamebrain, half-
wit son of theirs," Mr. Shinler snapped. "What's he
doing here?"

Tootie stiffened. It was all she could do not to shove
Mr. Shinler into the snow. He was no better than his
daughter!

The boy from the bus answered, "Well, sir, I thought
Olof would enjoy a change, so I'm bringing him to
school with me for a couple of days."

Donald McCarthy interrupted, "What a nice thing to
do, young man. We heard that country folks were kind!
Glad to see it! Things like this make strangers feel so
welcome. Already the people we've met have made us
feel right at home."

Arl nodded and led Olof back inside the bus.

Mr. Shinler frowned and ran his hands through his balding hair, which made the few remaining strands stand on end.

Tootie guessed that Mr. Shinler was trying to figure out just what Father meant by that comment.

The storeowner spit a stream of dark tobacco juice into the snow. Finally he turned toward Donald and pushed a piece of paper and a key into his hand. "Follow the bus."

Donald tipped his derby hat, put the key into his suit pocket, and glanced down at the directions to their farm. Then he walked over to the bus. "I want to follow you as far as here," Father said to the driver, and pointed to a place on the crudely sketched map.

"Got you!" the driver said with a smile. He was sitting inside the bus. The clear plastic flap that was usually the front window had been rolled up and strapped in place on top of the bus. The driver held a tight grip on the horses' reins, which came through the open space in the front of the bus.

Tootie had never been this close to horses. Icy fingers of fear and cold ran up and down her spine.

The curious students continued leaning out the bus windows, staring at her, Pearl, and their father.

"Carly Frank's my name," the bus driver shouted. "I'd shake your hand all proper-like, but as you can tell my hands are full." He pulled on the reins and the horses reared. He was a muscular young man, and it seemed to take all his strength to keep the team of horses under control.

"We'd better get a move on," Carly Frank hollered and then laughed at the frightened expressions of Tootie and Pearl as they backed away from the horses. "I want to get this bus across the tracks before the four o'clock flyer comes along." He threw back his head and laughed. "These broncos are hard to handle once they hear that train whistle!"

Then to Tootie's utter disgust, Carly Frank leaned almost out of his seat and winked boldly at Pearl.

Pearl giggled and winked back.

Tootie could hear some of the Siren students snicker. Then someone from within the bus began to chant "Carly's got a girl friend; Carly's got a girl friend."

"What next!" Tootie said. She grabbed her sister's arm, and she and Father led Pearl back to the truck.

The McCarthys followed the horse-drawn school bus down the icy road in silence. Neither of their parents scolded Pearl for winking at Carly Frank, nor did they say anything to Tootie about shoving Sylvia Shinler into the snow. Their attention was totally focused on the hazardous road ahead.

The only good thing about our introduction to this awful town, Tootie thought, *is that Buddy slept through it all.* She pulled him against her small frame and made sure he was wrapped securely in his brown blanket. *I'll keep you a secret, my Buddy Boy,* she promised silently. *Sylvia Shinler will never tease you!*

At the train depot, the bus glided easily across the tracks. Father ground the gears into low and proceeded slowly. They continued down the road for about a mile until Carly Frank pulled the bus to a halt to let off several students. After they climbed down the steps, they stood by the side of the road and stared at the McCarthys and their heavy load.

Tootie pulled Buddy closer.

Then about a half mile farther, the bus stopped again. This time Olof Olson and his friend, Arl, plus three more students who looked like brothers, got off. The three brothers hurried back to the McCarthys' truck.

"Your farm will be down that road," one of them said. "We're the Roy boys. We're your neighbors. Our place is on the other side of yours. I'm Lavern—the oldest. That's our little brother, Leo. And this is Lawrence." He slapped Lawrence on the back.

The three Roy boys smiled.

Just then Carly Frank leaned out the bus and waved. "Pick you up Monday morning. Right here! Seven thirty!" He pointed to the side of the road. Then he yelled to the horses, and the school bus jerked forward.

Father chuckled. "Have you ever—"

"No I haven't," Mother responded. "Do you think that bus is safe enough for our daughters to ride?"

"It's probably a whole lot safer than this truck," Father answered. Then he looked at the three brothers. "Nice to meet you," he said. He introduced Mother, Pearl, and Tootie. He pointed to Buddy, who was beginning to stir. "That's our little lad. He's not feeling too well." Tootie covered Buddy more securely.

The three Roy boys wore old dirty coats and rubber galoshes. Tootie thought she could smell manure as if they'd just come from working in a barn instead of from school. Even though the three brothers were different sizes, they looked alike with their stringy brown hair and dark brown eyes.

"The bus can't make it down these side roads," Lavern explained. He looked about sixteen. "So we always walk from here, don't we, Leo?" He slapped his youngest brother alongside the head.

"This is dreadful!" Pearl complained, wrinkled her nose, and stuck out her lower lip.

Lavern gawked and grinned as if he thought Pearl was the prettiest thing he'd ever seen. Then he pointed at Olof Olson. "You've already met him at the Mercantile."

Tootie's parents nodded.

Then Lavern turned and smiled directly at Tootie. "You sure showed that Sylvia Shinler a thing or two!"

Tootie fumbled with Buddy's blanket.

"And that's Arl Neilson," Lavern continued. "He and his pa work at the Olson place, right over there." Lavern pointed to a farmhouse off to the left of the road.

Arl nodded, tilted his hat, and stepped closer to the truck. "Thank you, Tootie, for trying to help Olof." He flushed as if just talking to a girl embarrassed him. His clothes looked as poor as the Roy boys, but they were clean. Tootie thought that somehow he wore his poverty with dignity. She watched as Arl dug the toe of his worn shoe into the snow. "Well, all I've got to say is thanks."

Tootie felt tongue-tied. And for the first time in her life, she could feel herself blush.

Father chuckled again. "Oh, our Tootie enjoys a good fight."

Mother interrupted. "We have this furniture to unload, Donald. We'd better get going. I'm anxious to see our new home."

"Why don't you all hop on the back," Father offered. "We'll give you a ride."

The Roy boys grinned, said "Thanks," and hurried to the back of the truck.

As Father turned down the side road, Tootie looked over at Arl Neilson.

"Do you want to hop on?" Father yelled over the noise of the engine.

Arl shook his head. "We don't have far to go." He took Olof by the hand and they walked away.

"That boy reminds me of your city friend," Father said and glanced at Tootie.

Tootie could barely swallow because of the big lump in her throat. She missed Joey so much!

Mother reached over and touched her on the arm. "God will have friends for you here, Tootie. And you too, Pearl. I just know he will because I've asked him for that very thing."

Pearl said with her nose in the air, "Who wants friends from this place? They smell! I hate it here! I want to go back home!"

"Now, now, lass, give it a chance," Father admonished. "Besides, you seemed to think that bus driver was all right."

Pearl couldn't help but giggle. "He was sort of cute. And he had such big muscles!"

"Pearl!" Mother admonished. "That's no way for a lady to talk."

"Oh, Mother." Pearl pouted.

The family got real quiet as Father carefully maneuvered the truck down the narrow country road. At first the tires spun, but the heavy load of furniture seemed to help. After about a half mile, the Roy boys yelled, "There's your place." They jumped off the back of the truck when Father stopped.

The McCarthys stared at a small rundown house without a lick of paint, sitting back off the road. Behind the house was a large barn. It was also bare of paint. Beside the barn stood something which looked like a shed for chickens. And beside the chicken house was the smallest little building Tootie had ever seen.

Mother said in a whisper, "Could that be an outdoor toilet?"

"A what?" Pearl said. "You can't mean—"

Father said loudly, "This can't possibly be the forty acre farm I bought." His voice and expression showed disbelief.

Lavern answered, "There are forty acres here all right, but most of it's swamp!"

"We bought swamp land?" Mother managed to say. Her complexion had turned a sickly white. "Forty acres of swamp?"

Leo answered, "Oh, Mrs. McCarthy, just the back thirty's swamp. We've even seen bears back there."

"Bears!" Mother exclaimed.

Pearl let out a high squeal.

Tootie pulled Buddy closer. He began to thrash about.

"I've taken care of Babe for you, Mr. McCarthy," Lawrence interrupted.

"Who?" Father asked.

"Babe, your cow. When Mr. Shinler told us that someone had bought the old place, I decided I'd better bring back the cow. She's in the barn."

"Oh . . ." Father said.

"We've got to go do our chores," Lawrence continued, and motioned to his brothers. "Pa will wonder where we are." He shoved his stringy hair out of his eyes. "Maybe we can come back tomorrow and help you unload your furniture."

None of the McCarthys could answer. All they could do was sit in their truck and stare in shocked silence at their future.

Buddy was the first to move after the Roy boys left. He stretched out of his brown blanket and began rubbing his eyes. Instantly the frown on his small round face turned into a huge grin as he looked out of the truck at the old farm.

Pearl burst into tears, and her fake front teeth moved up and down. "I hate it here!" she shouted and shook her head violently. Several pins flew out of her shiny black hair, and one tightly coiled bun hung loose over her ear.

"Maybe it isn't as bad as it looks," Father suggested. His voice sounded weak and tired.

"I'm sure you're right, Donald." Mother tried to sound reassuring. "A few coats of paint will do wonders to this place. And, Pearl, don't keep worrying about your teeth. Someday we'll get them fixed."

Pearl cried even louder.

"Come on, Buddy. Let's look around," Tootie suggested, knowing she had to get out of the close confines of the truck. As soon as she did, she took several slow deep breaths of the cold air. Then she looked up at the thick clouds still sprinkling snow. Making sure Buddy's wool cap was pulled down over his ears and his old coat was buttoned all the way to his neck, she said, "Let's go see Babe."

Buddy clapped his hands. "Babe! Babe! Babe!"

Tootie turned Buddy away before he could see the faces of their family as they got out of the truck, stood in the front yard, and stared in disbelief at the neglected farmhouse. Tootie and Buddy crunched through the snow to the barn.

The moment Tootie swung open the barn door, the smell of manure hit her full in the face. The barn smelled exactly like the Roy boys. Or did the Roy boys smell like the barn? Tootie plugged her nose.

But the stench didn't bother Buddy. He traipsed right in. A mouse scurried out of his path as he hurried excitedly toward Babe. The black and white cow was standing in a stall, chewing some hay. *A holstein*, Tootie thought, recalling pictures she'd seen of cows.

Buddy jumped up and down in his excitement and clapped his hands. Then he reached out and put his short arms around the cow's neck.

"Careful!" Tootie said and pulled Buddy away. Babe mooed contentedly. "I can see you two are going to be great friends." A smile touched Tootie's lips for the first time since arriving in Siren. And, for a brief moment, the angry expression in her eyes and the tightness around her mouth were replaced by a more gentle look.

She laid her hand on Buddy's shoulder and looked

lovingly at his bruised face. Buddy's expression reflected happiness for the first time in many months. "Babe! Babe! Babe!" he chanted and then took a handful of the hay that Lawrence Roy had left for the cow. Carefully he began nuzzling it close to Babe's soft mouth. The cow's lips folded over the hay and then she began to chew.

Buddy squealed with delight, rubbed his hands together, and grinned up at Tootie with his almond-shaped eyes.

"You're going to make a good farmer, Buddy Boy," Tootie said. Then the tenseness returned to her expression. "Let's go help unload the truck."

When they got outside, they noticed that Father had already backed the truck up, close to the front of their new home. Pearl and their parents were already inside. Tootie and Buddy hurried to join them.

The farmhouse was divided equally into four rooms—each 24 feet by 24 feet. The hardwood floors were bare and splintery, the plaster on the walls was peeling off in chunks, several windows were cracked, and one was completely missing. Part of that wall and the floor were water stained. Tootie stared at the flakes of snow floating lazily into the room. Then she pointed to the old square stove in the corner of the first room they had entered. It had a brick chimney running all the way to the ceiling. "I wonder if that works."

"It better," Mother said with a sigh. "That will be our only heat. And it's going to be a very cold night."

Tootie shivered and grasped Buddy's hand.

"By any chance, Tootie, did you see a stack of wood in the barn?"

"No."

"What about kerosene lanterns?"

"No. But I really wasn't looking."

"We'll have to find something," Mother continued. "This place has no electricity."

Father's shoulders sagged even more.

"What are we going to do?" Pearl asked, close to panic. She looked wide-eyed and her hair was still hanging loose on one side.

Mother put her arm around Pearl. "We're going to do what we've always tried to do . . . we're going to trust God."

The McCarthy family stood still, staring at one another.

"That's right," Mother continued. "And, we're going to ask God to help us deal with our anger." She looked directly at Pearl and then over at Tootie.

"You are angry, Tootie, because your reward money was spent on this." Mother spread her hands indicating the farmhouse. "And you're angry, Pearl, because you didn't get your front teeth fixed like you had hoped. Well, maybe your father and I are angry at being fooled by some false advertisement . . . "

Donald mumbled under his breath.

"This gives us all an opportunity to trust God," Mother continued. "And we can't really trust God until we come to terms with our anger. Don't let these angry feelings boil inside you. Get rid of them!"

How? Tootie cried silently.

Mother shook her head, deep in thought. "We all must guard against bitterness springing up in our hearts. Bitterness develops from disappointments such as this." Once again Eve spread her hands. "Bitterness causes people to become sharp, resentful, harsh, and totally unpleasant individuals. I don't want that to happen to anyone in this family."

Tootie bit down on her trembling lower lip.

Father had been leaning against the peeling plaster. He walked away from the wall and began dusting off his suit coat. Then he said in what Tootie thought was a very sarcastic tone, "My goodness, Eve, you've become quite the preacher!"

Mother's face turned pink. "Well, this trip has given me time to think, Donald. And I'm more convinced than ever that this move has the potential of bringing out the true character within each one of us."

Buddy wandered over to the stove and was fiddling with a knob when a side door on the stove opened.

"Look what Buddy found!" Mother exclaimed, obviously trying to change the subject. "I bet this is for storing water. How clever! When the fire's lit in the stove, the water will get nice and hot."

"What water?" Father asked in a disgruntled tone. "First we have to find a well. And if we happen to have one—it's probably dry." He turned and left the house.

"Poor Donald," Mother commented, "he's not used to all this."

"And we are?" Pearl burst into tears and ran out after her father.

Buddy hurried out of the house after them, yelling, "Babe! Babe! Babe!"

Tootie didn't say a word. All sorts of mixed-up emotions tumbled around inside her as she hurried to the truck and began unloading brooms, a stiff scrub brush, rags, and several buckets. Father hollered that he'd found the well. It was in the barn, in the front left-hand corner. He filled the buckets, and Mother and Tootie went to work. They swept and then scrubbed the old hardwood floors. Then they began cleaning out the stove. Meanwhile, Father, Pearl, and Buddy had scouted out the area. Father had found a small pile of wood, but discovered it was wet when he tried to light it in the cleaned-out stove. They couldn't find any lanterns, and the house soon became too dark to do any more work. The moon helped some, but it was still difficult to see inside the farmhouse.

Mother looked exhausted as she offered them the rest of the cold fried egg sandwiches. Everyone, except Buddy, refused. Tootie knew she couldn't eat a bite without it coming straight up.

After a hurried trip to the outhouse, they all tried to settle down for the night. Soon Tootie was lying between Buddy and Pearl on a mattress Father had brought in from the truck, before he'd driven the truck into the barn for safety. He and Mother had decided to unload only the mattresses and leave the rest for tomorrow. Besides, everyone was exhausted. They were going to sleep in their clothes, all crowded close together for warmth.

"At least the roof doesn't leak," Father said from the end of the row. He was lying on the other side of Mother.

"Thank you, God, for a good roof over our heads," Mother prayed out loud. Then she leaned up on one elbow. "I think that if we all thanked God for a few things, we would start to feel better about this whole situation. I've heard that when you give thanks to God, he begins to work. Who knows what will happen if we truly give thanks."

"Come on, Eve, that sounds like a bunch of blarney to me," Father responded.

Pearl yanked the covers over her shoulder and turned away from the family.

Tootie didn't want to give thanks. All she wanted to do was to bury her head in the mattress and cry. She was angry, hungry, cold, lonely, miserable, and totally exhausted from cleaning.

"I'll begin," Mother said. "I want to thank God for these mattresses. The floor would be mighty hard without them. Now, you next, Donald."

Father cleared his throat. He had never prayed out loud before. Although it wasn't quite a prayer, Tootie felt it came pretty close. He sat up and said, "I'm thankful we didn't slide into a ditch on the way here. That road was treacherous!"

Tootie was surprised that Father was being such a good sport.

Donald continued, "I'm also thankful that it stopped snowing and we could brush the snow off the blankets that cover the furniture on the truck. Also, I'm thankful we could drive our truck into the barn for the night."

Tootie immediately sat up and said, "I'm thankful that you found that old board in the barn and put it up against that broken window."

Mother added, "I'm thankful that Tootie is strong and that she could help me scrub this floor."

Buddy sat up and shouted, "Babe! Babe! Babe!"

Tootie and her parents chuckled.

Pearl said, while still curled up at the end of the row in a small ball, "I'm tired and freezing. Why don't we all be quiet and go to sleep!"

Just then they heard a noise outside.

"Do you think it's a bear?" Mother gasped.

"Not in the winter," Father replied with some confidence.

"Do you think someone's trying to get into the barn and steal our furniture?" Tootie whispered. The entire McCarthy family crowded closer together.

The noise became more distinct. It sounded as though someone were walking around in front of their farmhouse. Then they heard something land on the front porch and footsteps running away through the crusty snow.

"Donald, what should we do?" Mother asked.

Father got up and walked bravely to the door. After fumbling around for the knob, he yanked the door wide open. Immediately cold air gushed into the room. Then the wind caught the screen door and it flew open on its hinges.

There on the top step was a small pile of dry wood loosely tied together with baling wire. Father quickly picked up the wood and shut and latched the screen door.

Finally he leaned against the closed door and said in an awed tone, "Well, I'll be. Giving thanks wasn't blarney after all."

Mother replied in a practical manner, "I know God heard our thankful words. But I wonder who brought the wood?"

"Probably one of the Roy boys," Pearl said. "They kept staring at me this afternoon. Or maybe it was that handsome bus driver, Carly Frank."

"Well, whoever it was," Mother added, "we're thankful."

As Father lit the fire in the stove, Tootie pulled the blanket clear over her head. She had a lot to think about. *Had God heard their prayers of thanks? Or had it been the Roy boys? Or Carly Frank? What about Arl? Would he deliver dry wood to them in the middle of the night? Why?*

Tootie knew she should ask God to help her with her mixed-up feelings. But instead she bit down hard on her thumbnail. She wanted to believe that pile of wood had something to do with God hearing their words of thanks. *But,* she reasoned, *God probably doesn't even care what happens to us! He's probably forgotten all about us. If he did care, why did he let us move?*

Tootie ached all over, inside and out. She desperately wanted to know that God cared, and that he remembered them in this awful place. But somehow it seemed as though when they left their home in the city, they had left God behind.

I wonder if he even sees us all crowded together in this rundown farmhouse in Siren, Wisconsin? Tootie thought. She stuffed some of the blanket between her thin trembling lips to stop her crying.

The following day involved a lot of hard work. All the furniture and boxes were unloaded and everything was gradually put in its place. Father took a trip into town to get a couple lanterns, some kerosene, and even an ax to cut their own wood. Tootie had to admit that their farmhouse was beginning to take on a cleaner, lived-in look.

During the afternoon when Buddy was taking a nap, the Roy boys came to help. Thus far, no one in Siren had any idea anything was wrong with the little McCarthy boy.

I want to keep it that way, Tootie determined. *At least until his bruises are gone. I don't want to explain anything about his being in an asylum.*

Lawrence Roy demonstrated how to milk the cow. Everyone could tell that he was truly fond of the beast. Mother caught on quickly, but Tootie had a harder time. Father and Pearl wouldn't even try. Someone delivered another stack of dry wood on the porch Sunday evening, along with three big freshly caught fish. Speculations about who could be doing this kindness were discussed over the evening meal.

"I still think it's Carly Frank," Pearl said. "Didn't you see the way he looked at me?"

Mother shook her head. "Pearl, don't encourage that bus driver. Besides, he's too old for you."

Pearl stiffened. "Let me have a little fun in this awful place!"

Father interrupted. "Listen to your mother, lass. Remember the trouble you've caused in the past because of your choice of boyfriends!"

Pearl pushed away from the table and ran into the bedroom.

Mother sighed and took a card from her apron pocket. "I copied down a Bible verse this morning. I've read it a number of times today. I want to memorize it. Here, let me read it: 'Come to me, all you who are weary and burdened, and I will give you rest. Take my yoke upon you and learn from me, for I am gentle and humble in heart, and you will find rest for your souls. For my yoke is easy and my burden is light.'"

Eve put the card on the cherry wood table and looked thoughtfully at Donald, Tootie, and then at Buddy. "Jesus was a carpenter when he lived here on earth. I've been thinking . . . maybe he made yokes for oxen. Jesus probably knew just how to fit each yoke so it was tailor-made for a particular ox."

"Eve, what in the world are you talking about?" Donald asked.

"I'm talking about us, Donald. This whole situation!

It is tailor-made for us—the selling of our bakery, buying this farmhouse, the condition of this farm, even the timing of it— all of this was in Jesus' mind. And he has a purpose in it. This yoke, it's been tailor-made by a gentle and humble carpenter. He's allowed all of this to happen because he loves us!"

Donald quickly stood to his feet. The legs of his ladder-backed chair scraped against the hardwood floor. He mumbled something under his breath, and then a scowl crossed his face before he turned away and marched over to the sofa.

Mother sighed again.

Buddy took the last mouthful of fried fish, saying, "Mmmmmm!"

Tootie stared down at the card. She saw the words: "For my yoke is easy and my burden is light." It didn't make sense. Nothing was making any sense.

That night they all went to bed in silence.

Early Monday morning, the Roy boys arrived at their door. "We'll walk you to the bus," Lavern offered and smiled at Pearl.

Lavern Roy must have thought Pearl's pouting was pretty because he kept staring at her as if he'd never seen such a beautiful sight in all of his life.

Tootie grabbed her coat and red wool scarf. She hurried back into the bedroom and gave Buddy, who was still sleeping, a kiss on the forehead. Before she left the farmhouse, she said a quick good-bye to her parents. They were in a deep discussion at the table.

Neither looked up; they didn't even acknowledge her good-bye.

The Roy boys and Pearl were already at the end of the driveway. Tootie ran to them.

"Did you milk Babe this morning?" Lawrence asked the sisters.

Pearl shivered. "I can't even get near the beast!"

Lavern and Leo laughed.

Tootie answered, "I did." She and Lawrence talked about how much to expect from Babe and when's the best time to milk her. They talked until they came to the Olson's farm.

Arl Neilson came out of the house with Olof Olson. "He wants to come," Arl said and patted little Olof on the shoulder. "I hope Mr. Brightenger doesn't mind!"

"Or Sylvia Shinler," Lavern said and laughed at the look on Tootie's face.

"Are you going to shove her into the snow like you did last Friday?" Leo asked. "I loved it, Tootie! Do it again."

Tootie ignored the Roy brothers, but once again those angry feelings filled her heart. She looked at the little retarded boy. He had on an old oversized coat and was grinning proudly from ear to ear. *Why would anyone make fun of such a precious little boy?*

Just then the yellow bus, drawn by the team of wild horses, could be seen coming down the highway towards them.

"That crazy Carly Frank is really running them hard

this morning," Lavern said as he rubbed his cold hands together.

"Maybe he's anxious to pick up our new Siren students," Leo added and slapped his brother on the back.

The two brothers began shoving each other around in the snow until the bus came to a stop on its long metal runners. Arl moved close to Tootie and whispered, "The Roy boys are always fighting. At least those two. Don't mind them."

Tootie backed away from the wild horses and the tousling brothers. She was about to say something to Arl when Pearl grabbed her arm and whispered, "Oooooo, isn't he handsome!"

For a second, Tootie thought her sister was referring to Arl Neilson. But when she looked at Pearl, Pearl was blinking her eyes at Carly Frank. She held her lunch pail up in front of her mouth and peered over the top in a playful manner.

Carly Frank was sitting inside the school bus, with the open windows in front of him, grasping a tight rein on the horses. "Get on board, you little vixen!" he hollered to Pearl. Then he threw back his head and laughed.

Tootie didn't know what that meant, but she didn't like the sound of it. Nor did she like the way Carly Frank looked at her sister as she walked up the steps of the bus and slipped into one of the front seats.

Tootie hurried and sat next to her, as the Roy boys, Arl, and Olof filed to the rear.

The bus stopped several more times to pick up students before they finally arrived in the town of Siren. Tootie tried to talk with Pearl about school and what to expect from Sylvia Shinler, but Pearl was constantly flirting with the young bus driver.

As they crossed the railroad tracks on the outskirts of town, Carly Frank managed to slow the horses. Then he drove for about a block and pulled the team to a halt in front of the Mercantile.

Sylvia was peering out the store window. There were at least a half dozen students with her. Within seconds, the whole lot came hurrying out and onto the bus. Sylvia completely ignored Tootie and Pearl as she sauntered to the middle of the bus in her purple coat, hat, and gloves.

"When's your ma coming back?" Carly Frank hollered to Sylvia over the heads of the students.

Sylvia smiled at the muscular young man. Then she looked around as though she were on a stage and the students were the audience. She dramatically pushed aside a few black curls and said, "Shouldn't be much longer. Daddy says Mama's on a buying spree. I hope she brings me back a new coat. This old thing," and she patted the broad front of her purple coat, "is almost ready for the rag pile."

Pearl said in a low voice, "Well, I certainly wouldn't want to wear it."

Carly Frank leaned his head back and laughed so loudly that the horses reared. Several students, including Sylvia, went flying to their seats. He pulled on the reins, trying to regain control. Then he hollered over his shoulder, "Hold on everyone!" Finally the bus jerked forward, and it took all of Carly Frank's concentration to keep the animals from speeding down the middle of Main Street.

They pulled to a stop in front of the butcher shop to pick up a few more students, and then they turned onto Highway 35 for a short distance until they came to the school.

The brown brick building, which housed the Siren Consolidated School, sat back a distance off the road. The boys went in one door, and the girls went in another. The children from grades one to seven were taught on the first floor, and all the older students went upstairs. Pearl and Tootie followed. There were four classrooms for grades eight through twelve on the second floor. The eighth and ninth graders were in one room, and the rest had separate classes. The upper classes rotated rooms, depending on the subject matter being taught.

Lavern Roy hurried over to Pearl. "You're in my class," he said. "I'll show you around."

Pearl kept her mouth closed and giggled. She followed the oldest Roy boy without even a backward look at Tootie, who immediately noticed that Pearl's long underwear—which Mother had insisted on both of them wearing—was gone. Pearl had somehow rolled them up under her dress or had slipped them off when Tootie wasn't looking.

Lawrence Roy came over to Tootie and said, "Hang your coat over there," which Tootie quickly did. Then

Lawrence whispered, "Our teacher's name is Mr. Brightenger. He's—"

The rest of Lawrence's comment was lost when a man who was about five feet tall hollered, "Attention!"

The eighth and ninth graders jumped to attention and formed a straight line. Arl was protectively standing with Olof, not too far away from Tootie. He whispered, "Quick, Tootie, stand in front of us."

"Column right!" the small man hollered and the entire line turned right and filed into the classroom. Arl pointed to an empty seat in the front row, and then he marched to the back with Olof and sat down.

Tootie slipped into the seat and quickly opened her desk to put in her lunch. Suddenly the lid to her desk slammed shut right on her hand.

"Wait for the command!" Mr. Brightenger demanded. Then he frowned and deep furrows appeared between his dark eyes. "I don't know you. What are you doing in my classroom?"

"I'm new," Tootie managed to say. In no way was she going to show this mean little man how nervous she felt. She yanked her hand from under the desk lid and put them both in her lap. She'd stood up to the dreadful doctor and nurse at the asylum, and she could hold her own with this awful teacher.

"I wasn't informed that you were coming," Mr. Brightenger announced.

Sylvia Shinler raised her hand and swung it back and forth through the air. She sat two rows away from Tootie, and she impatiently kept waving her hand until the teacher looked her way. When he did, Sylvia said, "Excuse me, Mr. Brightenger, this is the girl who pushed me down last Friday. Her name is Tootie McCarthy. Her family bought that old farmhouse next to the Roys."

Mr. Brightenger pursed his lips and nodded. Then he began to cough. He almost doubled over in a spasm as he coughed and coughed. When it was finished, he walked back to the front of the room. Tootie noticed beads of sweat had popped out all over her teacher's face and down the back of his neck.

He picked up a book and pencil, totally ignoring Sylvia's comment, and began to take the roll. He called out one name after another. Sylvia glared at Tootie and then she leaned over to one of her friends and began to whisper.

Tootie felt like getting up, going over there, and knocking Sylvia right off her seat. Tootie wasn't paying close attention to the roll call until Mr. Brightenger called her name.

"Tootie McCarthy," he said without looking up from his attendance book.

Tootie didn't answer. "Tootie McCarthy," Mr. Brightenger said again, this time a little louder.

"Oh . . . present." Tootie answered as she had heard the others do.

"Arl Neilson," Mr. Brightenger proceeded.

"Present," Arl answered.

Sylvia interrupted, "And Arl's brought Olof Olson

with him again! I don't believe that stupid boy should be allowed to come to our school."

Mr. Brightenger didn't even look her way. He continued, "Lawrence Roy."

"Present."

"Leo Roy."

"Present."

"Sylvia Shinler."

"I'm here, Mr. Brightenger," Sylvia said. "And I still think you should do something about Olof Olson!" Sylvia glared at the retarded youngster. Then she smirked at Tootie almost daring her to defend the poor boy.

Tootie realized Sylvia was trying to pick a fight.

"Don't talk about Olof as though he can't hear you," Arl said.

"Come on—" Sylvia began.

Mr. Brightenger interrupted, "Enough of this. The young Olson boy can come to my class any time he pleases. He doesn't disturb a soul. Which is more than I can say for you." He looked at Sylvia Shinler. Then Mr. Brightenger began another spasm of coughing.

This whole incident seemed to increase Sylvia Shinler's hatred for Tootie. It was odd, but instead of her getting angry at their teacher, or Arl, or even little Olof, Sylvia glared at Tootie as though it were all her fault.

Several students noticed. Some whispered.

Tootie looked away.

The rest of the morning Tootie tried to concentrate on what Mr. Brightenger was teaching. But she found it close to impossible.

Could that Bible verse about the yoke being easy and the burden light include Sylvia Shinler? Tootie wondered and looked her way. *I don't think so!*

Sylvia lifted her balled fist and shook it at Tootie.

This time, no one else was looking. The rest of the students were doing the work in their notebooks that Mr. Brightenger had assigned.

Instead of looking away, Tootie glared back. Her heart began to pound. Suddenly Tootie forgot all about the Bible verse. She just kept glaring at Sylvia Shinler as though she was the cause of all the awful disappointments over the past few days. And the more she glared at Sylvia, the more angry Tootie became.

Sylvia mouthed, "You just wait!"

Tootie glared back, determined to wipe that smirk right off Sylvia's face.

Shortly after Tootie's and Sylvia's glaring match, Mr. Brightenger dismissed the class for their lunch break. Tootie hurried to the girls' lavatory without saying a word to anyone.

After she came out, she began looking around for the lunch room. *It must be on the first floor*, Tootie reasoned, wishing she had asked. On her way down the steps, she glanced out of the school window. It looked cold, and a few flakes were drifting down to the snow-covered ground.

Tootie stopped and stared. She felt so alone. *One week I'm at school in the city living in an apartment above our bakery. And the next week I'm here in the country at this Siren school living in an old farmhouse. And, to top it all off, there are people like Sylvia Shinler living here!* Tootie touched the cold windowpane. Her index finger traced $1000 on the cold, wet surface as she thought about her reward money.

I've got to snap out of this, Tootie chided herself. *And*

I've got to quit being so upset and angry. Am I turning bitter like Mama talked about?

Suddenly, out of the corner of her eye, Tootie saw something strange come into view: Sylvia Shinler was outside in the snow, leading little Olof by the hand. Sylvia was taking him away from the building!

"What is she doing?" Tootie asked out loud. "What's that girl up to now?"

Without taking time to think through the situation, Tootie dashed down the steps and out of the door. The cold air almost took her breath away and the breeze messed her short, reddish-brown curls into tangles. Her brown scuffed shoes slipped and slid on the hardened snow as she tried to run. Panic seized her. All Tootie could think about was the cruelty of the doctor and nurse at the asylum, and the way Sylvia had mocked little Olof last Friday.

She was about to round the corner of the school building when Arl grabbed her arm.

Tootie pulled away.

"Wait," he yelled, then stopped as he saw her expression. "What's wrong?"

"It's Olof!"

"Where is he? I was looking for him when I saw you run out here."

"With Sylvia," Tootie gasped. Then she turned the corner of the school and pointed toward Sylvia and Olof who were walking a distance away, over by a fence on the other side of the playground.

"What in the world!" Arl exclaimed. "What are they doing out here? It's cold!"

They watched for a few seconds. Sylvia was walking slowly by Olof's side along the fence which bordered a nearby farmyard. Then Sylvia stopped and pointed to something on the gate.

"Let's go see what she's showing him," Arl suggested.

But before he finished his sentence, Tootie was already running. She didn't know exactly why she was so filled with fear for the little retarded boy, but she was.

"Olof!" Tootie hollered.

Sylvia and Olof turned around. Even from this distance, Tootie thought she saw Sylvia's face turn a bright pink.

"Stop!" Tootie cried. "Whatever you're doing . . . stop!"

Arl quickly caught up with Tootie and they ran side by side. They saw Sylvia point again to the edge of the gate and try to push Olof's head down.

"What are you doing?" Tootie demanded as she came to a stop in front of them.

"Leave Olof alone!" Arl added. He too sounded outraged and out of breath.

"I wasn't doing anything," Sylvia defended. "Holey moley!" she exclaimed, "what are you two doing running after me! I was just being nice to this little fellow."

Sure, Tootie thought. Olof hurried to Arl's side.

"Are you all right?" Arl asked.

Olof just grinned. He looked happy and unharmed.

"Of course he's fine!" Sylvia shouted. "I just thought

he would like to see outside. I was showing him around! That's all!"

Tootie looked at the gate and the metal latch which closed it. "What were you trying to do?" she asked again. "You looked like you were pushing Buddy's head down."

"Whose?" Sylvia asked.

"Olof's!" Tootie corrected. "It looked like you were shoving Olof's head down into the gate."

"Why would I do that?" Sylvia stomped her foot in the hardened snow. "I was simply showing Olof some pretty snowflakes. How dare you!"

"We aren't accusing you of anything," Arl quickly interjected. "It just looked odd."

"Arl Neilson," Sylvia said. She appeared genuinely upset. "You and I have been friends for a long, long time. In fact, I count you as one of my very special friends." She tried to smile sweetly. Her pink-painted lips spread into a strained smile and her rosy cheeks puffed out. Her black thick hair curled every which way.

Arl frowned. "Well, I still don't understand what you're doing out here. Besides, you've never been nice to Olof before."

"Can't a girl change?" Sylvia pouted.

Tootie looked at Olof with his crossed eyes and simple, trusting expression. He was shivering. Tootie wanted to give him a hug and hurry him back into the warm school building.

Then she looked at Sylvia as she continued trying to convince Arl of her innocence. *Even if she does look ridiculous,* Tootie thought, *she looks like she's telling the truth. Maybe Sylvia Shinler actually was trying to be nice. Maybe I jumped to the wrong conclusion.*

"Sorry," Tootie said suddenly.

Sylvia looked at her in surprise.

Even Arl looked surprised. Then he smiled.

"Really," Tootie added. She stuck out her hand toward Sylvia. "I'm sorry."

Sylvia refused to shake Tootie's hand. Instead, she lifted her nose in the air, turned, and marched back to school.

"That was nice of you, Tootie," Arl whispered. Then he added, "But I still wonder if Sylvia's telling the truth. Do you really think she was trying to show him snowflakes?"

Tootie shrugged.

Arl put his arm around Olof to try to keep him warm.

Just before they left, Tootie looked once more at the gate and then the metal latch. She looked back at Olof. He was slobbering down his chin and his tongue was hanging slightly out.

What if Olof's tongue touched that metal? Tootie suddenly questioned. *It would stick. His tongue would actually stick to the cold metal! Sylvia wouldn't! She wouldn't dare! No one could be that mean!*

Tootie realized her imagination must be running wild. No ninth grader, not even Sylvia Shinler, would be that hateful to another human being.

As she, Arl, and Olof hurried back to the building,

Tootie didn't say a word about what she was thinking. It sounded spiteful even to suggest such a thing.

Arl opened the school door and whispered to Tootie, "I'm not going to bring Olof to school ever again. It's a lot of responsibility."

"It sure is," Tootie agreed wholeheartedly. She began to think back over the years of responsibility she had had over Buddy. She glanced at the tall, handsome figure of Arl as he dusted off the snow and rubbed Olof's arms to make sure the circulation was back.

I've found my first two friends, Tootie thought. A smile touched her thin lips. She decided to put all thoughts of Sylvia and her meanness behind her. *It's probably all in my imagination anyway*, Tootie reasoned.

Then she took Olof's other hand and all three of them hurried up the steps and into Mr. Brightenger's class.

Everyone was already seated when Tootie, Arl, and Olof walked into the ninth-grade classroom.

Sylvia said something to a couple of her friends who were sitting close by. They snickered and looked Tootie's way.

Mr. Brightenger said, "Attention!"

Tootie darted to her desk.

"Be on time," Mr. Brightenger demanded and looked directly at her and then at Arl and Olof who were hurrying to the back of the room. Their teacher immediately went into a spasm of coughing. When it finished, he wiped the perspiration off his face and neck.

"Sorry about that," he apologized. "I don't understand what's making me cough. Anyway, let us begin our first afternoon session. It will be on current events." Mr. Brightenger put his handkerchief back into his pants pocket. "Our country's economy has never been in such a state. People are spending entirely too much money. They are buying everything they can get their hands on."

"Like old farms," Sylvia said half under her breath.

Tootie wouldn't give Sylvia the satisfaction of looking her way.

"That's right," Mr. Brightenger proceeded. He acted as though Sylvia was adding vital information to the class discussion. "I don't believe that buying a farm at this time in our country's history is the wisest thing to do."

Arl raised his hand.

"Yes, Arl Neilson, do you have something to add?"

Arl stood to his feet. "Yes, sir. My dad and I have read in the newspaper about the farm bill that's before Congress. This bill promises that the government will pay for what the farmers cannot sell. If it passes, it will really help the hard working farmer."

"That is correct," their teacher said with a knowing smile. "But that bill has not yet been passed. This is certainly an interesting subject, one which I want to explore more fully."

Arl sat back down.

Mr. Brightenger almost went into another spasm of coughing, but he was able to stop it before it took control of his small frame. Then he announced, "Class, I have planned some debates. I've made a list of subjects. And being that this is a farming community, the farm bill happens to be on my list. Arl Neilson, since you show such interest in this area, I wonder if you would like to take this subject?"

"I sure would," Arl said.

"Good. What position do you want to defend, and who do you want to debate?"

Arl stood to his feet again. "I would like to take the position that the bill should be passed by Congress. I also want to show how this bill will help farmers. And I'd like Lawrence as my debating partner." Arl nodded toward his friend.

"Lawrence Roy, is that all right with you?" their teacher asked.

Lawrence stood by the side of his desk. "It sure is! We'll get a real good debate going."

Mr. Brightenger wrote their names on the blackboard as Lawrence sat back down.

"The upcoming Presidential election will be the next debating subject," their teacher continued. "Who would like to take the position that President Calvin Coolidge should run for another term of office?"

Several students volunteered.

Tootie was hoping she would be excused from the debates. They sounded interesting, but she didn't know all the rules. She'd never had debating at her last school.

Just then Mr. Brightenger announced the next subject. "Here is an interesting one," he said. "Asylums. I want to hear a good debate on asylums: their proper use, who should be admitted, so forth and so on." Tootie sucked in her breath.

"Miss Sylvia Shinler," Mr. Brightenger said. "Here is your chance. You are always harping on the retarded being kept away from normal folks—or whatever it is you keep saying. Here is your opportunity to do some study on the matter. You can look up about asylums, what goes on in asylums, and who you think should be admitted."

"Yes! Yes!" Sylvia said. "I want that subject." She stood and glanced at little Olof who was doodling quietly on a piece of paper. "I think every last one of them should be locked up!"

"Now, now, save that for your debate. Who would you like to choose as your opponent?" their teacher asked.

"Tootie McCarthy," Sylvia stated with confidence. She looked at Tootie with challenge.

"Who? Oh, the new girl." He glanced at Tootie. "You take the opposite viewpoint or position. I want you to defend the right of the mentally ill to stay in our society in these modern times of 1928."

"I really don't want to," Tootie began. "Honest, I've never been in a debate before. I really don't know all the rules."

"You'll learn!" Mr. Brightenger said. "I pride myself that every ninth grader, before he passes my class, must learn how to debate properly. And, I might add, I want you to also note that the rule in this classroom is that you stand whenever you address the teacher."

"Yes, sir," Tootie said, quickly getting to her feet.

"That's better." Mr. Brightenger turned toward the blackboard and wrote Sylvia's and Tootie's names next to the subject of asylums.

"Don't worry," someone from the back of the room whispered loudly. "Tootie can hold her own."

Another student added, "Remember last Friday? She

and Sylvia already had their first debate. And Tootie won!"

A number of students laughed.

"Attention, class! What is all this whispering?"

How can this be happening? Tootie wondered as she sat back down and stared at her tightly clasped hands. *I don't want to be in a debate about asylums—especially with Sylvia Shinler!*

Meanwhile, their teacher had gained control of the class and was proceeding to give instructions. "I want each one of you to do thorough research on your subject. Go to the library. Check out books and look through newspapers and magazines. Of course, we don't have our own newspaper here in Siren, but we do get a number from the surrounding towns—especially Webster. You can even interview people or take a census in the community on your subject. You'll be graded on how you support your viewpoint. Debates will begin this Friday."

Tootie could feel her heart pounding in her temples. *Newspapers!* she thought in desperation. *Surely Sylvia won't find that article in* The Tribune—*it's from Minnesota. But what if she does? What am I going to do?*

The next couple of days were awful for Tootie. She dreaded the upcoming debate, and the tension was becoming almost unbearable. Sylvia tried to pick a fight with her at every turn. Pearl continued flirting openly with Carly Frank, giving people much to gossip about. Mother's health continued to improve with every passing day, but Father became more and more resentful of the farm and all the work involved. The tension between their parents was obvious. Buddy was the only truly happy member of the McCarthy family. He played constantly in the barn, learned how to milk Babe, and was forever talking with the gentle animal. As the week progressed, there were times when Tootie wondered if she might indeed be turning into an angry, bitter person. It wasn't so much what she said—because she tried to keep her mouth shut—but it was the horrible thoughts constantly flying around in her head.

"What's bothering you?" Father asked as he passed her one evening with a pile of crudely cut wood in his arms. He dropped the load into the box by the stove, then dusted himself off with his clean white handkerchief. He still wore his dark suit every day. Tootie thought it looked ridiculous and out of place on the farm.

Tootie looked up from the books and newspaper articles she'd checked out from the library. She'd been doing a lot of reading on asylums. The whole subject brought back such terrible memories.

"Nothing," Tootie responded and quickly looked back down.

There were no newspapers from Minnesota in the small school library. That fact should have encouraged Tootie, but she still felt all tied up in knots.

"You're sure acting mighty strange for someone who has nothing bothering her," Father commented.

"I do have a lot of homework," Tootie offered.

"Oh, is that all?" Pearl interrupted. She was sitting at the table next to Tootie. She kept staring at her reflection in a piece of mirror which she'd propped against the kerosene lantern. "Just look at my front teeth," she moaned. "When am I going to get these fixed?" She tapped her fake front teeth with the tip of her fingernail and looked reproachfully over at her parents.

"As soon as we can," Mother promised. She was cleaning up after their fried potato and onion dinner.

"There are still so many things we need for this farm," Father interjected. Then on a lighter tone, he added, "By any chance did either one of you see what your little brother did this afternoon?" He smiled at Buddy who was sitting on a small scatter rug, fiddling with his shoes.

Pearl shook her head indicating that she hadn't seen what her brother had done nor was she particularly interested in hearing about it.

"Buddy found an old oxen yoke in the barn," Father explained. "It was among some of the useless farm equipment left by the previous owners. Anyway, Buddy learned—all by himself—how to put that yoke on Babe. He had that cow pulling a log around in the snow this afternoon in our front yard. It was the strangest sight!"

Tootie wished she could have seen it. It was wonderful how Buddy was enjoying the farm. Then she thought about her mother's comments concerning a yoke, and how this farm was like some sort of a handmade yoke for their family. And that Jesus had somehow arranged this move because he knew it was the best for each one of them. The whole idea of this yoke being easy and the burden light made no sense. The only one that was adjusting to the move was Buddy.

Tootie shut her books, picked up all her school work, and hurried into the bedroom.

Finally Friday morning arrived. From the moment they stepped into the school bus, Pearl began flirting shamelessly with Carly Frank. No matter what Tootie said, Pearl ignored her. Tootie wanted to hide under the seat because she knew Arl, the Roy boys, and all the other students were watching.

Before long, Carly Frank glided the bus to a stop in front of the Mercantile. Sylvia Shinler and the students who had been waiting with her by the potbellied stove, hurried out and into the bus.

Sylvia glared at Pearl when she passed. Then she stopped in front of Tootie and pointed her purple-gloved finger right into Tootie's face. "Your sister had better quit distracting our bus driver! I told Mama all about how Pearl McCarthy's been acting."

Carly Frank laughed loudly and then reined in the horses. "Don't worry, I can handle it." He winked at Pearl.

Pearl giggled.

Tootie didn't know who she was more disgusted with: her sister or Sylvia Shinler.

Just then Lavern Roy hollered from the back of the bus for all to hear, "Come on, Sylvia, you're just jealous of both of the McCarthy sisters!"

"I am not!" Sylvia defended.

"You are, too," Lavern continued teasing. "Carly Frank's in love with Pearl. And then our friend here, Arl Neilson, brings piles of wood and has even caught a fish or two for Tootie and the rest of her family. All in the name of love!"

Lavern slapped Arl on the back and laughed at his flushed face.

Tootie also blushed.

Sylvia's look was one of raw hatred. She glared angrily at Tootie. Her pink-painted lips curled into a snarl. "You just wait for our debate. You and your sister won't be stealing all the boys in town when I get through with you."

"Oh, sit down," Carly Frank demanded. "We've all heard enough of your threats!" He yelled at the horses and the bus jerked forward.

What in the world did Sylvia mean? Could she possibly have found out the truth about Buddy and the asylum? How? Oh, God, Tootie prayed silently, feeling close to panic. *Help!*

Immediately after taking roll call, Mr. Brightenger wanted to start with the debates. He looked excited. "Class, let's begin with the debate between Arl Neilson and Lawrence Roy on the farm bill. Come up here you two young men. Arl, you stand on the right. And, Lawrence, you take your position over there behind that podium on the left."

Mr. Brightenger had arranged the room to accommodate two podiums in front, on opposite sides of the blackboard. It was obvious to Tootie that debating was a serious matter to their teacher.

Tootie had not had a chance to talk with Arl and thank him for the wood and the fish. She knew he was embarrassed, but she still wanted to tell him how much she had appreciated it. His acts of kindness had really helped their entire family during their first days in Siren.

Sylvia Shinler had basically tried to ignore Tootie after Lavern's teasing comments in the bus about the McCarthy sisters stealing all the boys in Siren. Sylvia also didn't say anything more about their upcoming debate, and some of Tootie's fears began to subside. She knew that *The Tribune* article from the big Minnesota newspaper was nowhere to be found in their small Wisconsin town.

Tootie began to relax as she listened to the debate. Both Arl and Lawrence did a good job of presenting their views on the farm bill. Tootie thought Arl's points were stronger, but Lawrence also presented the opposite view very well.

Mr. Brightenger congratulated the two.

Then Arl said, "The reason this bill is so important to me, is that my dad and I are saving to buy our own place. If this bill passes Congress, we'll go ahead with our plan."

"Wise thinking," Mr. Brightenger said. "Well, young man, good luck! I hope the bill passes and all works out for you and your pa."

Throughout the remainder of the day, the debates went on. Mr. Brightenger took time out for some mathematics and he also gave them a list of spelling words to work on for Monday. Shortly before school was to end, he looked at the big face of the clock above the door and said, "I think we have time for one more debate."

Tootie held her breath.

Pointing his chalk at the list on the blackboard, he went on, "Asylums. Let's hear the debate on asylums. Sylvia Shinler and Tootie McCarthy, come forward please."

Mr. Brightenger indicated the place where Sylvia was to stand, and then motioned for Tootie to go to the other podium. Tootie's heart pounded as she straightened her notes and placed them on the wooden stand. She didn't look up.

"Now," Mr. Brightenger said, "I will flip this coin to see who begins."

"Oh, let Tootie go first," Sylvia said. "I don't mind." She smiled sweetly at the teacher and then at Tootie.

Could I have been wrong about her? Tootie wondered. She knew it was a real advantage to speak first because Mr. Brightenger's rule was that the one who began the debate was also the one who would end it with a few closing remarks. His method of debating didn't seem fair, but Tootie wasn't about to mention it now—especially with Sylvia's generous suggestion.

Tootie took a deep breath to calm her nervousness. "Asylums," she began, still looking down at her notes. "Even the word strikes fear into the heart of the strongest individual!"

Then she looked up. Arl was smiling at her, so was Lawrence, also a few other students. Those smiles helped. Even Mr. Brightenger nodded his head, indicating he liked her opening statement. Sylvia also nodded in an interested fashion as though she wanted Tootie to continue.

"Through my research, I have discovered that terrible, unbelievable things go on behind the locked doors of an asylum. Patients are mistreated. They are given rotten food that even animals couldn't eat. Sometimes patients are stripped of their own clothing and made to wear uniforms, which are often covered with lice."

Several students moved uncomfortably in their chairs. Even Mr. Brightenger looked up from his note-taking.

Tootie continued, "I have also read that the patients in an asylum are punished in terrible ways. They are beaten for all sorts of little things. For instance . . . maybe they accidentally wet their pants."

Someone snickered.

"Anyway," Tootie continued, "all sorts of things like this upset the people running asylums. They also use something called a wet pack. How this works is they soak long strips of canvas material in water. Then they take the mattress off the bed, put the patient on, tie him tightly to the bare boards with the wet material. As the material dries, the patient is pressed closer and closer to the wooden slats."

Tootie was thinking of poor Buddy when she had found him at Fairbolt. He'd been put in such a contraption and left for hours. She remembered the pain in his face.

"Also, in some asylums, an electroshock machine is used." Tootie went on to tell how a patient is strapped to a table and how the wires from the machine are attached to the patient's head and body. She then told very dramatically how the machine is turned on and bolts of electricity are shot through the patient.

Several girls in the classroom screamed, and one girl looked close to fainting. Even Mr. Brightenger turned pale.

"I've read that these electric shock treatments are still in the experimental stage," Tootie reported. "Someday, the experts say, they may be useful. But now, in 1928, we do not know enough about them to be using them in our asylums. They are not being used to help patients, they are presently being used to punish them."

Everyone was listening with complete attention.

"I believe," Tootie began her concluding remarks, "that some people need to be locked up and kept away from society for their own safety and for the safety of others. But there are very, very few individuals like this. And if we do continue to put these people in asylums, our government needs to enforce strict rules. Nobody should be mistreated. And I also believe that there are many people in asylums today who should not be there at all. They are slow mentally, but most of them are gentle and trusting. They would never harm a soul. They are special people. People like Olof Olson."

Arl smiled broadly.

"Remember, this is 1928," Tootie ended. "We should treat people with dignity and respect. Each one of us should learn to reach out in kindness to people like Olof who are different. They should not be locked away in some terrible place like an insane asylum. If we would just give them a chance, we could all learn a lot from these special people."

The entire classroom clapped when Tootie finished. Even Mr. Brightenger nodded his approval before he called the class to order. Then he indicated that it was Sylvia Shinler's turn.

"Do you believe what you've said?" Sylvia directed her opening statement at Tootie in a sincere tone.

Tootie stared at her. *What an odd way to begin her side of the debate.* "Yes," Tootie answered. "I believe every word I said."

Suddenly Sylvia's innocent expression turned into an ugly sneer. She shook her black curls away from her face. "Then why are you hiding your brother?" she demanded. She pulled out *The Tribune* article and picture from her notebook and held it high for all to see. "Mama came back from shopping in the big city. And just look what I found wrapped around some of the new dishes she bought."

Tootie's knees went weak. She held onto the podium for support.

"This girl, who just talked to all of us with such conviction, is hiding her dumb brother out at that old farm! He's run away from an insane asylum!" Sylvia shook her finger at Tootie, "And she helped him escape!"

Everyone in the classroom sat stunned. Tootie could hear several people gasp, but no one said a word.

Sylvia paused, allowing time for the news to sink in. Finally she continued in a hushed, almost ominous tone. "The McCarthys were probably run out of the city. And now they've come here to our quiet little town, thinking they can hide their shame." Sylvia pointed to the picture of Buddy with his tongue hanging out and bruises all over his face. "This boy, Buddy McCarthy, is dangerous. Just look at him! Now we will all have to start locking our doors at night. Siren is no longer safe . . . not with the McCarthys around!"

Mr. Brightenger walked over to Sylvia and took the

article. Then he looked across the room at Tootie. "This is you all right, Miss McCarthy. What do you have to say for yourself? Is this boy, standing in the middle, really your brother? Was he in an asylum?"

Tootie didn't know what to say. Sylvia had totally misrepresented the whole thing.

"Answer me, young lady," Mr. Brightenger demanded. "Is this your brother? Was he in an asylum?"

Tootie held her head high.

"Well?" he persisted.

"Yes," Tootie answered. "But—"

Before she could explain more, the bell rang.

Mr. Brightenger quickly announced, "Class dismissed!"

The students stood to their feet and began to file out of the room. Sylvia held up the picture of Buddy as they passed. Several looked Tootie's way in disgust, and one girl squealed, "I'm scared with someone like that on the loose. Will we be safe?"

"He's just a boy!" Arl defended, after he'd seen the picture. He walked over and stood next to Tootie. "I bet Olof would like to meet your little brother. They could be friends." Arl said it loud enough for all to hear.

Tootie quickly gathered her books. She and Arl walked to the bus together. The Roy boys joined them. Pearl was already there, sitting in the front seat directly behind Carly Frank.

Tootie could feel her forehead and temples throb with every beat of her heart. She didn't want to sit with her sister and watch her flirt. And she definitely didn't want the entire busload of students staring at her and her sister as they talked about Buddy and their fears.

She held her head high, marched past Pearl, past Sylvia who was still grinning, and proceeded down the aisle to the whispers and stares of dozens of students. Finally she slipped into the seat next to Arl by the rear emergency door.

All the way into town gossip about the asylum debate was being whispered from one row to the next. No one said anything to Pearl or to Carly Frank, who were totally preoccupied with each other.

Tootie could imagine how the story about Buddy was getting bigger and bigger as it was passed from one student to another. She wanted to stand up and tell them how sweet Buddy could be and that there wasn't a mean or dangerous thing about him.

I'm not ashamed of my Buddy Boy, Tootie wanted to cry out so everyone would hear it from her own lips. *I just didn't want any of you to tease him—especially Sylvia Shinler!*

But it was too late. No one would understand now. How could something so innocent as trying to protect her brother be turned around like this? Tootie had never felt so wretched in all of her life. The bitterness in her heart threatened to bust it wide open.

I'll get even with Sylvia Shinler, Tootie promised herself, *if it's the last thing I ever do.*

To Tootie's relief, they finally reached town. Carly Frank pulled the horses to a halt in front of the Mercantile. Mr. Shinler was peering through the dirty front windows of his store. He hurried out to the school bus as soon as it stopped.

"Sylvia," he hollered. "Your ma's gone back to the city. Says she forgot a few things. I'm going after her before she spends all my money!"

"Pa!" Sylvia exclaimed.

"Don't Pa me!" Mr. Shinler shouted into the bus. "I want you to go to one of your friends for the night."

"But Pa!" Sylvia whined as she stood to her feet in the aisle of the bus and shook her head at her father. "I couldn't possibly stay at anyone's house. I'll need something to wear!"

"We'll wait," Carly Frank hollered as he tried to keep the horses in check. "I don't mind holding the team here for a short while—they're acting mighty skittish. But don't take long." Instead of hurrying, Sylvia sauntered slowly into the Mercantile with two of her friends. They were obviously fussing over which of her friends' home Sylvia would choose.

"Hurry up!" Carly Frank shouted.

Arl pulled out the list of spelling words for Monday. "We might as well learn these. I think those girls are going to take their time."

Lawrence turned around and leaned over the back seat. "I need to get home. We've got chores."

"Me, too," Arl said.

Tootie felt thankful that neither of them talked about the debate, nor did they ask any questions about Buddy.

Tootie couldn't concentrate on their spelling assignment. She just stared out at the town around her.

Sylvia took a long time. And the longer they waited, the more restless the horses became.

Pearl giggled. "Ooooo, look at your muscles, Carly. They bulge way out!"

The young bus driver had his coat sleeves pushed up almost to his elbows, and Pearl kept pointing and squealing at the large muscles on his forearms as he tried to keep a tight rein on the horses.

Carly Frank hollered for someone to go get Sylvia.

Just then, Sylvia came out of the store with a bundle in her arms. Her friends were also carrying several sacks. Sylvia stumbled up the bus steps and landed in her seat. She didn't even thank them for waiting.

The bus swiftly pulled away from the curb onto Main Street, heading out of town. Then to Tootie's horror, she saw Pearl lean forward and kiss Carly Frank on the back of his neck. He turned around and said something to her.

Others must have seen it too because several students pointed.

At that very moment the four o'clock flyer blew its whistle from up the track. It spooked the horses so badly that they took off at a mad run. Carly Frank tried desperately to gain control, but it was too late. There was nothing he could do. The horses ran straight for the railroad tracks.

"Help!" Pearl screeched.

"Help! Help!" others added.

"We're going to die!" Sylvia Shinler bellowed.

Panic gripped everyone in the Siren school bus. Some flung their arms in the air, screaming. Others hugged friends, while a few sat as though frozen in place.

Arl grabbed Tootie's arm and pulled her to the floor.

Tootie could hear the constant blowing of the train whistle and the scraping of the runners on the bus as they began to cross the tracks. The sound was deafening. The bus started to swerve from side to side. *If the bus tips over, we'll all be killed!* Tootie thought.

Just then the bus cleared the tracks, and the train zoomed past barely missing them. But Carly Frank still could not gain control of the frantic horses. They sped forward, pulling the bus down the highway, jerking the passengers violently from side to side. After what seemed like hours, the horses veered off the road, pulling the unwanted load across an open field. Eventually the runners must have hit something hard, because it sounded as though the bus were being ripped apart. The emergency door popped open. Tootie and Arl were still on the floor, clinging to the bolted down frame of the back seat. It was then that the bus tipped over on its side. The cold, hard ground passed only inches away from Tootie's face. Just then the bus spun around. The bolts came loose and the back seat, along with Tootie and Arl, spewed out the rear door.

About fifty yards farther, the big yellow bus came to a complete stop.

Silence.

The sudden shocking silence sent chills through Tootie's thin body. She looked over at Arl with wide frightened eyes, and then they both got up and started running toward the bus. The horses were nowhere in sight.

By the time Tootie and Arl reached the accident, they could hear whimpering and a few cries.

"Pearl," Tootie screamed. "Pearl, are you all right?" In a frenzy, Tootie tried to peer into the bus.

"I'll find her," Arl promised. "You run for help."

Tootie stared at him.

"Hurry! This is the marshland behind your farm. The ground's frozen—so nothing's going to sink. But hurry!" Arl demanded again. "Get help! I'll start pulling people out."

Tootie started to run. *Is Pearl all right? Is anyone hurt?* All these thoughts kept racing through her head as she ran across the frozen acres to her farmhouse.

Her legs were so wobbly that she stumbled several times before she finally reached the farmyard.

"Help!" she gasped. But her voice was too weak for anyone to hear.

The sound of wood being chopped came from the other side of the barn. Frantically, Tootie ran toward the noise. "Help," she cried again.

Just then Buddy rounded the corner of the barn. He was leading Babe. He had put the yoke on the black and white cow and had her pulling a sled full of chopped wood.

Mother came running out of the farmhouse.

Father let the ax fall and hurried to catch his daughter. "What is it, lass?"

With gasping breath, Tootie explained what happened. They all rushed into the barn and soon gathered together the old blankets which had been used to cover the furniture when they moved. They tossed them onto the open back of the truck, along with all the rope they could find. Father was cranking up the engine, when Eve called, "I'll have everything ready when you return. Bring the children here." Father and Tootie stepped up into the cab of the truck and were leaving the yard, when Tootie saw Buddy and Babe.

"Stop!" Tootie yelled. "If people are hurt real bad, we might have to use that as a stretcher!" Tootie pointed to the sled piled high with wood.

"That would work!" Father exclaimed. "Have Babe pull it!"

Tootie jumped out of the truck, waved her father on

toward the site of the accident, and immediately began flinging the wood off the sled.

When she tried to lead Babe, the animal would not budge. "You've got to help," Tootie cried to Buddy. "Make Babe come."

Buddy touched the cow's soft muzzle and began to walk. Babe followed.

It was slow going. Dozens of times Tootie wished she had gone back to the accident with her father and had never come up with this idea. She tried her best to explain the situation to Buddy. He didn't understand as he looked over at her and grinned in his sweet, simple fashion. The bruises on his face that he'd received at the asylum were beginning to fade.

Tootie couldn't believe how quickly everything had changed. Here she was leading her brother to the bus accident—right into the crowd of Siren students who had been gossiping about him just minutes earlier.

By the time they arrived, most of the frightened students were out of the bus, hovering close together. Father and Arl had taken charge of the situation. The younger children were already seated in the back of the truck, covered with blankets.

Tootie immediately spotted Pearl standing by herself, not too far away from the bus. She was cupping her mouth with her hands and crying uncontrollably. Tootie left Buddy and Babe and ran to her.

"What's the matter?"

Pearl looked up with grief-stricken eyes. She pointed

to her mouth and then back at the bus. "My teeth!" she cried.

"I'll find them!" Tootie promised, wondering how in the world she was going to find Pearl's plastic plate with the attached teeth in all that mess.

Soon everyone but Sylvia Shinler was out of the bus, either by their own efforts or with the help of other students. They had dozens of cuts and scratches and all of them were going to be extremely sore in the morning, but no one was badly hurt—not even Carly Frank. All he seemed concerned about was his stupid horses. He darted off in the direction he thought his horses had gone. He didn't even stay around to help, nor to check on Pearl.

Father, Arl, and Lawrence Roy were lifting Sylvia out one of the windows of the bus. She still had not come to.

Meanwhile, Tootie had climbed inside the bus, looking everywhere for Pearl's front teeth.

"What are you doing?" Father asked in surprise. "Quick, Tootie, have Babe pull that sled over here. We're going to need it!"

Tootie hurried out of the bus. She and Buddy encouraged Babe to move closer as everyone watched.

Someone yelled loudly, "Hey, that's Buddy. That's the boy from the picture—the one that Sylvia showed us!"

"Is he the boy from the insane asylum?" someone asked, close to hysteria.

"Look!" Arl hollered. "Calm down! He's just a little boy . . . and he's helping us!"

Lawrence added, "And look what he's taught his cow to do!"

Just then Sylvia moaned.

By that time, Father, Arl, and all three of the Roy boys were carefully but hurriedly laying Sylvia on the sled. Buddy encouraged his cow to pull forward and take Sylvia away from danger.

Sylvia looked pale as she lay bundled in her huge purple coat. She moaned again. Father began to tie her securely to the sled so that she wouldn't be able to move during the journey to the farm. Tootie added a blanket.

"Is she going to die, Mr. McCarthy?" one girl asked.

"No! Not if we can help it!" Donald replied. "She probably has a concussion. I don't believe she has any broken bones, but the truck ride would be too rough for her."

Tootie interrupted, "So my brother's going to help. He's going to take Sylvia back to our farmhouse. My little brother is helping in the rescue. Right, Buddy Boy?"

Buddy grinned at the gawking students and then at his cow. "Babe! Babe! Babe!" he shouted. Tootie hugged her brother for all to see. "I'll go with you."

"I'm coming, too," Arl added.

"And the rest of you, pile back into the truck," Father said. "And cover up good and warm with those blankets. We want no one coming down with pneumonia."

As everyone hurried back to the safety of the truck,

Tootie saw Father take Pearl aside and hand her something from his suit pocket. It was wrapped in his white handkerchief. *Her teeth! Father's found Pearl's plastic front teeth!*

Pearl quickly put the plate in her mouth. Then she looked over at Tootie and smiled. It was the prettiest smile Tootie had ever seen.

"Let's hurry," Father said to everyone. "I'm sure by now my dear wife has some hot soup on the stove and a nice cozy fire."

For Tootie, Arl, and Buddy, the walk to the farmhouse was indeed slow. Babe had a hard time pulling her load, but Buddy encouraged her all the way. He constantly repeated her name, while gently rubbing and patting her.

Tootie looked at Arl several times and then away. Finally she mustered her courage and whispered, "Thank you."

He looked over at her, "What for?"

"For the wood, the fish, for just being my friend!"

Arl stared down at his old shoes.

"I'm glad Lavern told me," Tootie continued. "I've been wondering who God used to answer our prayers. You've been like a mysterious helper to our family."

Arl looked up. "I wanted to help. And your brother, Buddy, is another mystery helper. In fact, we could call him the mysterious rescuer!" Arl smiled at Buddy and then looked over at Tootie. "No one will forget what he's done today!"

Tootie agreed. "And I don't think anyone here in Siren will ever be afraid of him again."

Then Tootie looked down at the sleeping form of Sylvia Shinler and whispered, "Please, God, help Sylvia!" It was surprising. The moment Tootie prayed for her enemy, her angry feelings toward her began to leave.

Sylvia uttered a low groan.

It was almost dark by the time they arrived at the barn. Everyone hurried out of the farmhouse to see how Sylvia was doing.

"I was just coming to find you," Father greeted.

"How is she?" Mother asked, trying to get a closer look.

"I think she's waking," Tootie said and then stepped back. As she looked around, she was surprised to see how much better everyone appeared. Most of the students had already been washed and bandaged. *And they're probably full of Mama's hot soup,* Tootie thought. Her stomach growled.

Eve knelt close to the sled. Father was kneeling next to her holding the kerosene lantern high. Everyone crowded around. Even Buddy.

"She's so pale!" someone said. One of her friends began to cry.

Just then Sylvia opened her eyes. "Wh-wh-what's going on?" she stuttered in her confusion.

"Lie quiet," Mother admonished.

Sylvia ignored her and tried to sit, but the ropes held her tight. "Get me out of this thing, you stupid people!" Sylvia cried. "What are you trying to do to me?"

"Hold still, little lass," Father said to Sylvia in a smooth tone. Then he pointed up at the hind end of Babe, which was only inches away from Sylvia's head. "Don't rile that animal, or there's no telling what she may do!"

"Do . . . do . . . do," Buddy added and grinned directly into the face of the unthankful girl he'd just helped rescue.

Sylvia took one look at Buddy in the light of the lantern and screamed at the top of her lungs. "Holey moley! Get him away from me!"

It was odd, but for the first time Tootie didn't feel like yelling back at Sylvia.

"Don't talk like that to little Buddy McCarthy," one of Sylvia's friends said. "He's the one who rescued you!"

"That's right," Lawrence Roy added. "Buddy and his cow, Babe!"

Sylvia glared. Then she continued struggling, trying to untangle herself from the ropes, and slapping everyone who attempted to help.

Tootie watched. Gradually, more and more of her bitter feelings against Sylvia began to slip away.

Then Tootie looked at her father who was thoroughly enjoying watching the entire scene. He glanced Tootie's way, smiled, then winked.

Tootie winked back.

Mother stepped close to Sylvia. "You should be thankful, young lady. You could've been hurt. And for pity's sake, quit thrashing about like this!"

As Mother continued scolding Sylvia, Buddy walked to the front of Babe and began whispering into her ear.

Tootie joined him. She put her hand on the yoke as she watched Buddy gently touch the cow's soft wet muzzle.

Pearl came and stood next to Tootie. She smiled gently. "I saw what you did, Tootie. You went back into that bus to find my teeth."

"I'm so glad you've got them!"

"Thanks," Pearl whispered. "This accident has really made me think."

"Me, too," Tootie said. Immediately the Bible verse, "My yoke is easy and my burden is light," came to Tootie's mind. She felt overwhelmed and surprised by her thoughts. "We fit here!" she whispered. "Our family fits here in Siren . . . on this farm. God really does know what's best for each one of us!"

Buddy said tenderly, "Babe . . . Babe . . . Babe," and kept patting his cow.

"I'm hungry," Tootie suddenly said. "Come on, Buddy, let's go get something to eat."

Pearl asked with a mischievous look, "Are you going to save any food for that spiteful Sylvia Shinler?"

Tootie looked at her and smiled. "Yes, Pearl, believe it or not, I'm actually going to save her a bowl of soup. And I'll even save some for Carly Frank . . . whenever he returns with those awful horses."

"Oh, Tootie, do you really think he's coming back?" Pearl asked hopefully.

Tootie stared at her sister. Then she put her arm around Pearl's shoulder and swung her other arm around Buddy. Their parents joined them. The McCarthys walked into their farmhouse together.